STRAIGHT UP

The Autobiography of Arthur Daley
as told to
PAUL ABLEMAN

William Heineman Ltd
Michelin House, 81 Fulham Road, London SW3 6RB

LONDON MELBOURNE AUCKLAND

First published in 1991
Novel copyright © Paul Ableman and Leon Griffiths
1991
Minder scripts copyright © Leon Griffiths 1979–85

ISBN 0 434 00066 3
A CIP catalogue record for this title
is available from the British Library

The author has asserted his moral rights

Typeset by Falcon Typographic Art Ltd
Edinburgh & London
Printed and bound in Great Britain by
BPCC Hazell Books, Aylesbury, Bucks

CONTENTS

Photographs supplied
by Thames Television
and Stephen Morley

PREFACE

IN THE PAST I HAVE often been asked why I have never written my autobiography. Modest to a fault, I have always replied: 'Surely no one would be interested in the memoirs of Arthur Daley, even though his early struggles and later triumphs resemble, and in some ways transcend, those of such famous tycoons as John D. Rockingfellow and all them Rothschilds?'

On being assured that I was wrong, and that I am known admiringly in local business circles as the Onassis of SW6, I have still backed off and, mindful of the amount of work involved in writing a book, contented myself with a faint smile, a modest shake of the head and the quietly spoken words: 'Naff off. I've got better things to do with my evenings.'

But then about a year ago a conversation occurred which made me rethink my attitude. This chinwag took place in The Winchester, a club which I patronise where, in tasteful surroundings, local businessmen such as myself can discuss their affairs. Knowing my reputation, you will perhaps be surprised to learn that this momentous exchange of views was not with the mayor or some local bigwig but with none other than the sterling fellow called Dave who is the barman and owner of the club.

I was, in fact, enjoying my customary early evening vodka and slimline and Dave was studying, with furrowed brow, a tabloid newspaper on the other side of the bar, when he suddenly looked up from his paper and, out of the blue, asked:

'Ever think of writing your memoirs, Arthur?'

I am admiringly known in local business circles as the Onassis of SW6

'Not you too?' I asked with a sigh. 'Why is it that all the illiterates in this manor are bent on enslaving me to a typewriter?'

'There's an item here,' Dave explained, 'about how Simon Capstick wrote a book of memoirs. Seems he made fifty big ones out of it. And that don't count the movie.'

Clutching the bar for support, I exclaimed: 'What, Slimy Capstick? The dwarf that flogged battery-operated kittens down the Tube station?'

'That's him. Went on to bigger things – shifting counterfeit Swiss watches in Oxford Street. And now he's written his memoirs.'

'Memoirs?' I interrupted crossly. 'The only memoirs Slimy Capstick could have would be of scarpering whenever he saw a flash of blue approaching.'

'Anyhow,' urged Dave diplomatically. 'Seems his book sold a hell of a lot of copies. Capstick got his own back on the coppers what used to harass him and all. Because of his allegations, two of them have been suspended. Straight up, Arthur, I reckon if he could do it, so could you.'

I sighed once more and observed:

'I certainly can't see Simon Capstick wielding a pen with more *savoir-faire* than me, and that's a fact.'

'You could write better too,' Dave said. 'I think it could be a very interesting book – all about the tricks and shady deals you get up to and –'

'Hang about!' I cried indignantly. 'I'll have you know that my business methods have never been impugned.'

'Maybe not, Arthur,' agreed Dave. 'But some people say they're a bit dodgy. Anyhow I wasn't thinking so much about all your wheeler-dealing. I was thinking more how you know this manor better than anyone and you could write a – well, a kind of history of it. You know, describe Fulham as it used to be and how it's become –'

I nodded, still a little miffed by Dave's attitude.

'Yeah, well – I may give it some thought, when I've got a free moment. Meanwhile, just have a care with your allegations, Dave.'

'Oh gawd!' he exclaimed anxiously, peering down the front of his trousers. 'Have they come loose again?'

Well, a free moment did come along and I gave it some thought. The factor that weighed most with me was, as Dave had suggested, the chance to put down some of the history of my beloved Fulham. Because it is quite true that I know a lot about it. Take people. Straight up. I have met them all. I doubt if there's a single tea-leaf or nutter – or even the rare honest

Dave noses into my affairs

trader – that's ever so much as passed through the manor that I haven't had some dealings with. From my trusted colleague, one-time contender for the world heavyweight title, Terry McCann, to the scummiest street pedlar like Slimy Capstick, I have definitely known them all.

And what's more, I went on to thinking, it's not only people, it's also places that I could share with my readers. How many Londoners are aware, for instance, that there's a tunnel connects the basement of the White Hart in Broadhurst Street with a certain wharf on the riverbank? It was used in days of yore by smugglers trying to elude the customs cutters and offload French Brandy and Portuguese Port. I have even used it myself, not for smuggling, naturally, since that is a dishonest activity, but for the discreet shipment of certain continental merchandise which, to avoid the ludicrous and trade-stifling bureaucratic practices which so bedevil the common market, I elected to shift at night in high-speed ocean-going launches that showed no lights. When they built the new leisure centre they blocked up the tunnel without realising what it was or where it went. But it's still there and if anyone who reads this book can think of a good use for it, I could, if I approved of his scheme and the price was right, show him how to dig through to it again.

£*I am one of those rare men who can never be really happy unless he is making others happy*

Yes, I think the chief reason why I gave Dave's proposal so much consideration was the thought of how much pleasure I could provide for my readers by my unique knowledge of Fulham and its byways. The truth, which causes so much head-shaking and anxiety amongst those who have my economic best interests at heart, is that I am one of those rare men who can never be really happy unless he is making others happy. This is a quality that is sadly lacking in much of today's business community and my possession of it is another good reason why I was increasingly drawn to the idea of this book.

For some weeks I toyed with these, you may feel, rather noble thoughts. Moreover, I am by no means ashamed to admit that Dave's words about the financial rewards that could flow from the production of a good autobiography also gave me food for thought. The truth is that although I have been famous all my life for my carefree attitude to lucre, and my utter indifference to my own bank balance when there is any charity or good cause requiring my unstinting support, it is still as a businessman that I come before you in these pages. And what is the market credibility of a businessman if he cannot turn a profit or seize a golden opportunity? Dave had compelled me to realise that a book of memoirs might prove to be a very nice little earner indeed.

After all, if a pavement pollutant, to put it mildly, like Slimy Capstick could bank a cool fifty grand from parading his reeking reminiscences before the public then what was to prevent me, a cultivated and literary personality, from turning out a tome that would stoke up a Swiss bank account? Nothing that I could see. I mean, could Capstick enrich his puerile prose, as I have done over and over again, with tasteful quotations from the Bard? Could he buggery! For the Capsticks of this world bard is what happens when you get Brahms and make a right Charley of yourself in some boozer.

It goes without saying, I am sure, that my plans for the utilisation of the Niagara of bees and honey that I saw buzzing delightfully from my book turned chiefly on benefiting those in the community less fortunate than myself such as widows and orphans. Nevertheless, as all sensible people know, charity begins at home and naturally my generous heart contemplated before all other worthy causes what my increased fortunes could mean to 'er indoors. For some years now, she had whispered to me tenderly but incessantly that our old three-piece suite was little better than a housing estate for Bonny Dundees and asked pathetically why we couldn't have a new one from Harrods or some other posh shop. I confess that a tear of joy formed in the corner of my eye as I imagined her delight when the delivery van rolled up with a gleaming new Draylon three-piecer. I was also ecstatic at the thought of delighting her with a few little luxuries like a case or two of Babycham and a few jars of the pickled walnuts to which she is so attached.

In the grip of such delightful plans and schemes, I negotiated the purchase, at a very keen price, of an almost-new portable typewriter from a foreign businessman eager to restore friendly relations after a little disagreement over the value of some merchandise had induced me to ask Terry McCann to go round and reason patiently with the fellow.

Bearing this state-of-the-art machine home in the boot of my executive Jaguar, I immediately flexed both my index fingers and set to work. Well, it has taken me the best part of a year but now my task is done and a monument to human literary genius is ready to be set before you.

Just one thing saddens me as I prepare to send this book off to the publishers and ultimately into your living room. This is that my dear friend and colleague, Terence McCann, whose forceful business methods have won respect throughout Fulham, will not be here to share with me the excitement of publication. Each man must seek his star and 'Tel' has, after much reflection, decided to honour Australia with his presence. The offer of participating in an exciting business venture there has lured him from our shores. Our loss is, of course, Australia's gain and one of the very first copies of this masterpiece will, you may be sure, soon be winging its way to the distant continent where my old minder has gone to seek new triumphs.

Ray's professional qualifications include a punch like a battering ram

And who, you may be wondering, will replace him in my life and business activities? It is, in fact, a chap called Daley! No, I am not going to stop keeping a dog and do the barking myself. I refer to a strapping young fellow called Ray Daley, a nephew actually, who has all the qualities of the man he replaces, including a punch like a battering ram. So good luck, Terry! We will never forget you. And the next instalment of my memoirs, which all you readers are certain to demand, will feature a new team, Arthur and Ray Daley. Straight up.

ARTHUR DALEY
FULHAM
1991

CHAPTER ONE

A FAMILY OF DISTINCTION

The Daleys, for nearly a thousand years, produced an unbroken line of top people

Y OU WILL PROBABLY be astonished to learn that I am only the latest in a long line of over-achievers. Originally of Celtic stock, we Daleys, at the time of the Norman conquest, acquired a good dollop of Norman blood, and the combination proved unbeatable. From William the Conqueror's time to the present day, the Daley clan has spouted every imaginable kind of celebrity. Statesmen, poets, industrialists, jockeys and many others have been, if I may put it so, plums on the family tree. Since even to list them all would be the labour of months, I must content myself with mentioning just one or two of the most eminent. Amongst these is Major-General Daley who, in the eighteenth century or thereabouts, put down an uprising by some native tribe in Darkest Africa and then patriotically snaffled up its land for the good old British Empire. I must also find space to recall the artist, Rupert Daley, who was a celebrated pre-raffleite painter (meaning that his canvases were snapped up for cash and never needed to be raffled like those of lesser daubers) and whose divine works hang today in such places as the Louvre in Paris.

In his treatise: 'The Daleys of Fulham and England', Marcus Patel, the well-known Fulham genealogist, lists no fewer than four earls, seven barons and a whole clutch of lesser nobs as belonging to one branch or another of the far-flung Daley clan. There is also a prime minister in there and any number of professors and pugilists. In short, to really know the Daleys is to know England.

Certain unkind voices have whispered that Patel was merely a mercenary hack, trying to ingratiate himself with me to stop me prosecuting his dishonest old dad who owed me for a superb vintage Toyota he had driven away from my yard on tick. But this is untrue. I hired Patel to research my ancestors long before I flogged the Toyota to Patel senior. Others have alleged that a week is hardly long enough for young Patel to have thoroughly researched my origins but the lad had three A-levels, one of them in history, and knew his onions when it came to family trees. As proof of his talent he now writes the column on astrology for the *Southall Gazette*. His mother was an air hostess and met his father eight miles up over the Indian Ocean. Case of love at first flight.

Anyway, Patel has proved beyond reasonable doubt what family tradition has always maintained: the Daleys, for nearly a thousand years, produced an unbroken line of top people. And then this magnificent sequence was tragically cut short. What by? You guessed it: by the horrors of the First World War. It was in this cruel and muddy struggle that my paternal grandfather, the Honourable Desmond Daley, died a hero's death in the trenches.

Already an Oxford don, which is very different from the Brooklyn kind, at the astonishingly early age of twenty-eight, the Hon. Desmond, upon the outbreak of hostilities, volunteered for active service and was soon dispatched as a subaltern to the Western Front. There his bravery became legendary and led to a colonel of the staff, scarlet from wine-bibbing, saying to a general one day: 'If you really want to capture that salient, sir, you'll have to send either a squadron of them new tanks they've just invented or young Daley.' Unhappily, the general chose the latter and Gramps perished leading the assault. He left behind him a young

*My grandfather,
the Honourable
Desmond Daley*

wife and a six-year-old son.

Now, of course, there was no welfare state in them days and my grandmother was very soon destitute. You may wonder why she did not apply for a widow's pension or seek immediate help from her wealthy in-laws and the truth necessitates at this point admitting to a skeleton in the family closet. Although this skeleton will seem minor and even endearing by modern men and women of our permissive age, it was held by the stern morality of them days to be truly shocking. My grandfather and grandmother were never legally hitched. This was because the Daleys had considered my grandmother, although the pious and honourable daughter of a wise old country parson, beneath them, and had threatened to disown my grandfather, and thus deny him his share of the huge Daley fortune, if he married her.

So grandfather was dead in no-man's-land and my grandmother was left with a six-year-old son, my future father, to raise and not a bean in her pocket. She applied to all the usual charities and received a few hand-outs of old clothes and such-like rubbish. Finally she even demeaned herself by pleading on hands and knees to the proud Daleys for help but these curs spurned her and that is one of the reasons why I myself, to this very day, carry a charge of burning scorn for my ancestors and hardly ever mention them in conversation. Merely to recall my grandmother's suffering causes my face to darken and my eye to flash dangerously. My silence about my origins is, of course, the reason why so few of my friends have even the tiniest inkling about my glittering ancestry and there are even ignorant pigs in this parish who regard me as nothing but a jumped-up guttersnipe. What clowns they would feel if they knew the truth!

So there they was, this tiny, forlorn family consisting of a beautiful, well-born young woman and a helpless child. What could they do? To whom could they turn? The cruel world streamed past without so much as turning its head or proffering a crust. Normally, of course, any son of the Daleys would have been all set for the finest and most costly upbringing England could provide. But none of this largesse beckoned for little Arthur (that's right – I was named after my dad). Not for him some expensive prep school followed by Eton, Oxford and the Guards. Instead, and at a tender age when a lollypop or cuddly bear would have been more appropriate for his little dimpled hand than a bunch of filthy brushes, he had to go out to work as a chimney sweep just like Tom in the classic kiddies' book 'The Water Fairies'. It was hard, backbreaking toil clambering up the sooty stacks but so proud was little Arthur of being a support for his mum that there are old men in Fulham who, to this very day, recall the black imp whistling as he swung home through the streets at dusk to the single grimy basement room which the forlorn pair

Trade in the trenches

called home. But however ragged was his dress, my grandmother always made sure that little Tom – that is, little Arthur – had plenty of plain but nourishing fare to help him grow big and strong. There was none of your high-fat, low-calorie junk food on their rickety kitchen table. I recall Dad telling me once that he was in his thirties before he ever set eyes on a hamburger.

The result of all this wholesome food was that Arthur soon grew too big to get up chimneys.

He was offered instead the post of messenger to a firm of accountants based on the old Blackbird Tavern in Charteris Square. Young Arthur used to convey messages from clients detailing their investment requirements and his employers would then invest the specified sums at the racecourse. This form of financial enterprise was, in them days, rather ridiculously considered by the authorities to be unlawful and dodging the rozzers gave Arthur an alertness and knowledge of the best steps to take in an emergency which was to serve him in good stead when he finally began his own business career.

It was early in the thirties and my dad was just coming up to his twenty-first birthday, when he at last had a spot of real luck. It came about because of the increasing use, offensive to the democratic instincts of all true Englishmen, of informers, plainclothes detectives and other provocative agents by the police. Since you couldn't scribble a betting slip without having a hand come down like thunder on your shoulder, the Blackbird Tavern became an unsafe place for Arthur's employers to conduct their popular and lucrative enterprise. Casting about for a more secure location from which to operate, the firm hit on the idea of buying a small shop which ostensibly had nothing whatever to do with nags thundering over the turf. The one they hit on was an ironmonger's (as they was known in them days) and it was now that Arthur's experience as a chimney sweep came into its own. Since he had some idea of the kind of things that should be available in an ironmonger's shop he was appointed manager. Of course, he was not really expected to sell much in the way of chimney sweeping equipment or boot polish but rather to take betting slips which he could do under the very eyes of the prowling Old Bill. However, to the surprise of his colleagues the shop soon began to flourish in its own right.

Arthur was by this time allowed a share of the overall profits and within three years these had piled up and he was able to make an offer to buy the place. Since two of the bookies had been arrested for practising a sideline, which was armed robbery, and given long prison sentences and the third one had drunk himself to death, my father found himself, at only twenty-five, a fully-fledged ironmonger with a small but well stocked establishment in Fulham High Road although not at the fashionable Chelsea end.

But sadly he had very few friends. His ex-business partners were mostly in the nick and so, desperate for human companionship, he took to spending time in the old Brigantine Tavern in Lowther Street. Gradually he spent more and more time there until in the end he was always the first one in at opening time and the last out after the licensee bawled: 'Last orders, gentlemen, please!' Even worse, he took to taking bottles of whisky home with him to the small apartment above the shop. As a result he was Brahms most of the time and his business began to suffer. Who wants to buy ironmongery from a red-eyed bloke, breathing hard, who blinks blearily at you from behind the counter? Very few people. So Dad's debts began to pile up and that made him guzzle even more to block out mounting worries about money. Heaven knows what might have become of him but for the fact that the Brigantine acquired a new barmaid.

The first time she smiled at him and asked: 'What'll it be?' in her becoming Irish lilt, my dad knew that this was the only girl for him. He gazed at her round, pretty face with its shining brown eyes beneath delightful peroxided ringlets and thought: 'I'm going to marry this girl.' I know this because Dad told me about it many years later in Woolworths where he was buying Mum a tenth anniversary present. So he started to court her seriously.

I am not a teetotaller but I always use the firewater cautiously

Although a trifle seedy and downtrodden, as well as being a near-illiterate from lack of schooling, my dad nevertheless had in him the easy, debonair confidence of Daley bucks down the centuries. So even as he took delivery of a large whisky and water from Marjie's soft hand, he grinned and asked:

'What's your name then?'

'Marjie Rawlings,' answered my mother-to-be.

'Thought you was Irish?' suggested my father mischievously.

'And why would you think any such thing?' asked my mother-to-be playfully, exaggerating her natural Irish accent out of sheer merriment.

My mother went on to explain about her studies at the Lolly Lipstick School of Beauty and Cosmetics and my dad listened attentively. He then suggested that he pick her up after school and they might go somewhere and take a bite together. My mother, attracted by his bold, cavalier manner, readily agreed.

But that night she was disappointed to find how

much he drank. He got totally elephants by the end of the evening and she informed him that she didn't like drunks and wouldn't ever go out with him again.

So began a struggle which was to last for many years and which haunted my childhood. I myself am well-known in Fulham social circles for my moderation in the use of alcohol. I am not a teetotaller but I always use the firewater cautiously. I may take a cocktail or a medium-sweet sherry before dinner, and for purposes of everyday refreshment I use wholesome vodka and slimline tonic. I am also fond of fine wines, and have been complimented on having a superb palate by leading wine experts such as Benny French who, under the pseudonym of Old Bacchus, for years did the wine column in the *West London Chronicle*. But when a bottle of, say, the artful '75 Château Dominic or the hilarious '82 Bournemouth White (one of the few British wines that can hold its head up in foreign company) comes my way, I still take no more than a glass, or possibly at the outside two, with my fish supper. Perhaps once or twice a year, say at a dinner of the Rotarians, I may unbend a little and reach home not quite as Gibraltar-like as usual. But it is never a rolling-pin scene. 'Er indoors has never been driven to express her reproaches by anything more forceful than, say, an affectionate shake of the head or slightly-pursed lips as she propels me firmly towards the staircase and bed. Well, by now you've probably guessed what I'm getting at. It was the spectacle of the suffering and anguish of my father all through my childhood, as he strove to stay sober, that has given me such a mature and responsible attitude to the River Ouse.

Naturally, when my future mum expressed disapprobation for my father swilling like a Russian that first time they went out together, he immedi-

My father struggling to stay afloat in the River Ouse

ately swore that he'd give it up then and there. And the thing is that he really meant it and he tried hard and, to some extent, he succeeded. He didn't take a drop for weeks, maybe months, after that first date, and by the time his restraint snapped and he went out and got totally Brahms once more he and Mum had forged a bond that was to prove strong enough to bear the strain of the difficult years to come.

The inability to stay dry was the reason why my dad never had a decent career. What happened was that my mother took over the failing ironmonger's shop and turned it into a beauty salon. She soon proved herself a first-rate beautician and also a good businesswoman and would probably have ended up with a chain of shops and become rich except that so much of her energy went to looking after her kids and her old man. I am the oldest but I have three sisters and two brothers, most of them in places like Canada and Australia now. But my mum's little shop was one of the landmarks of Fulham and it was this that kept us all well fed and clothed in childhood.

It was more than a year after they met before my mum and dad got married. They loved each other from that first moment Mum slid the large Scotch across the counter into my dad's eager hand but the River Ouse which had brought them together also kept pushing them apart. My dad proposed time and time again during that first year but always, just as Mum was softened up and ready to accept, he'd go on another binge and blow his chances. It was touch and go as to whether they ever would tie the matrimonial knot but then something happened which made it almost certain that they would. Yes, you've guessed it. Mum got pregnant. Yours truly was on his way.

CHAPTER TWO

EARLY DAYS

D ID NAPOLEON TODDLE ABOUT his sand-pit with
one hand stuck in his vest and the other
pointing towards Russia? Did Shakespeare scratch
away with a chalk on his toy blackboard? Did Sir
Christopher Wren build little cathedrals out of his
play-bricks? Unhappily we do not know. But we
are lucky in having detailed knowledge of the
early days of at least one human being bound
for greatness. For by asking around amongst those
who knew me as an infant, and from my own first
memories, I know a great deal about what my
own childhood was like.

It is strange how often earliest memories seem
to be a kind of prediction of a person's later life.
I have found, by making enquiries, that this is true
in very many cases. Take Dave, our beloved host
down the Winchester Club. His earliest memory is
of drinking a glass of some delicious fluid – ninety
proof Ribena, very likely! Toddy Gimlett, the tea-
leaf what specialises in nicking cars, remembers
just that: nicking a toy car from another toddler
who set up a hell of a shindig and chased him
on all fours. But the funniest early memory of
all was Terry McCann's. He was boxing with his
dad and actually knocked his old man out cold!
Straight up, little Tel, just able to walk, KO'd
his pa. What really happened was that his pa, a
big bruiser and well-known amateur boxer, was
crouching down getting Terry to throw punches at
him and suddenly, just as the little fist connected
with his chin, a half brick, which the older McCann
kept as a paperweight (or so he claimed in court),

*£ The
only Sony
Walkman
CD players I
will handle
are made
by a firm in
Dundee which
produces the
finest Sony
ringers on the
market*

fell off a shelf and clouted him on the bonce, laying him out cold.

In the same way, my earliest memory points in the direction of my great achievements in later life. It is of standing in my cot and throwing out rusks that had a nasty taste. My mum has since told me they was flavoured with liquorice and this seems likely because ever since I have detested the flavour of liquorice. So what was the connection between an infant throwing rusks and a man who towered over his fellows because of his financial genius? It is the quest for quality. Neither the infant nor the man was prepared to put up with a junk product. Nowadays if I get a consignment of dodgy goods from some jumped-up firm I simply will not touch it. Recently, for example, I was offered a consignment of Sony Walkman CD Players made by a basement firm in the East End of London. I rejected the offer with indignation. The only Sony Walkman CD players I will handle are made by a firm in Dundee which produces the finest Sony ringers on the market.

*Me, testing a
rusk for quality*

My earliest memories also point very clearly to the courtly and dapper man I became. I remember, for example, sitting on the laps of a great many pretty ladies and hugging and kissing them. These was the customers in Mum's beauty parlour and they vied with one another for the privilege of having me on their laps. In fact, so keen was the competition that Mum sometimes made me the prize in her 'clear skin' competitions. The lady who looked after her skin best, and who came in for her session with the most velvety and glowing epidermis, was allowed to have me on her knee to neck with. Of course, the necking was all very innocent but I can remember to this day the delight of stroking and patting and snuggling into the laps of all these charming women. And, of course, as we snuggled and playfully groped we engaged in delightful badinage. The women would cry, 'Ooh, you naughty boy! You mustn't put your hands there!' And I would squeal with delight and retort, 'But that's where it's nicest, Mrs Tomkins', or something along those lines.

From my mum and her beauty parlour I gained that deep understanding of the gentler sex and its needs which brought me such success with women in my young manhood and which, since then, as 'er indoors would eagerly confirm, has made me into a model husband.

Another very important series of early memories is of being taken to parks and gardens in Fulham and even further afield. On Sundays, sometimes, the whole family went to Kew Gardens and I remember the terrific impression it made on me. I would gaze up at the great trees from all over the world and exclaim, 'Coo, look at that one', or, 'Crumbs, you can't see the top of this one', and it bred in me that deep understanding of nature which I have retained to this day and which is why people that come to my home always congratulate me and 'er indoors on our splendid collection of pot plants.

Just potty about pot plants

Now, in spite of the joy I took in Kew Gardens and other London parks as a child, I have to admit that I am basically a city person. My idea of the Garden of Eden is Piccadilly Circus on a Saturday night. I am not an enthusiast for great stretches of wilderness. But I think it was the respect for nature bred in me by my parents which is the reason why I am completely at home in rural circles when circumstances take me there. I can bounce along in the back of a Range Rover with a labrador seated beside me, in my plus-fours and deerstalker, just like any of the country set. This was demonstrated, as it happens, only about a month ago when I took a consignment of Italian tiles to the delightful estate of Sir Horace Bickersley, Bart, in Wiltshire. After depositing the tiles, I was pleasantly surprised when the baronet said:

'Don't know if you're free tomorrow, Daley, but if you are perhaps you'd care to hunt?'

'Well, I should get back to London. Hunt what?'

'Oh, a fox or two if we're lucky. Haven't caught a glimpse of one for months, actually. You ride, of course?'

'Oh, of course. But I haven't brought my saddle with me.'

'We can provide a mount. Hunted before, have you?'

'Naturally. In fact there was a time when I practically lived on horseback.'

'The ground's good – pasture and some rough. What do you say?'

'Nothing I'd like better. Always gives me a thrill, pounding across country with the sound of the horn echoing in my ears and the hounds yelping – but I think I'll give it a miss.'

'Pity.'

'It's 'er indoors. She worries, you see. Knows how I can never resist a good hunt. If I was to break an arm or a leg she'd never forgive me. But if you like I could stay and cheer you on.'

'Oh no. Only put temptation in your way. Well, thanks for the tiles. I'll send you my cheque.'

'Couldn't you write it out now?'

'Like to. But I broke my finger hunting. I'll let you have it when the bone mends. Doctor chappy says it shouldn't be more than a month or so. Sorry, you can't join us tomorrow. Cheers.'

That's just an example of how easily I can fit in with country life when I need to. I'm a pretty handy gun too and think nothing of bringing down a rocketing pheasant at fifty yards with a Purdey twin-barrel. But for all the delight I am capable of taking in the countryside I still regard any place that is not covered in buildings as a bit beyond the pale.

I was just four when the Second World War began.

We soon found that life wasn't all that different from in peacetime except that you needed all your wits about you to get enough sweets because the ration was pathetically inadequate. A quick gulp of sherbet or a nibble of Fry's Chocolate Cream and that was your lot for the week. Unless, of course, you had devised ways of separating the other kids from their rations.

One of my own first attempts along these lines was by manufacturing my own ration coupons at home using crayon and exercise-book paper. Naturally I was not, even at them tender years, thick enough to try and use my home-made coupons on shopkeepers. What I did was offer my little playmates two weeks' worth of my home-made coupons for one week's worth of the kind put out by the Ministry of Food. Although I had yet to reach my seventh birthday my sales pitch was even then so convincing that loads of kids flocked round to get a piece of the action and my pockets were full of delicious things again. I only came unstuck when angry parents began complaining to Mum. She was so embarrassed when she found out about my enterprise that she gave me one of the very few spankings she ever administered, although even then she couldn't bring herself to make it really hurt. I learned an important lesson from this venture: if you've got some dodgy commodity you want to shift, remember you've not only got to convince your customer that it's a good buy but the customer's mum and dad as well. In other

Everything was rationed including sweets

But I want to stay with you, Mum!

words your merchandise has got to be of good enough quality to satisfy everyone what's likely to get close to it.

Now in 1939, Desmond and Gloria, my kid brother and sister, was too young to be separated from their mother but I was put down for evacuation. In due course, I watched Mum disappearing down a station platform (or so it seemed although it was really me disappearing up the track) and burst into tears as the understanding fully dawned on me that being evacuated meant being separated from Mum. I was still gulping a good bit when we chuffed into the simple wooden station of Lower Pendle in West Somerset on one of the branch lines that Beeching has since axed and where I was supposed to pine away the war years separated from my beloved mum.

I was lodged with the village draper and his missus and they had three kids of their own, all in their teens and so sod-all use as company for me. But the whole family was very kind and made me the family pet. I went to the local school and have no bad memories of that either. But you won't believe this: in the whole time I was in Somerset I never understood a word anyone said to me. This was because they did not speak English but a strange language a bit like Robert Newton playing Long John Silver only much more incomprehensible. They would point and say something and laugh and I'd just stare at them because I hadn't got the joke. So my time in Somerset was not specially sociable.

But it did give me my first real experience of the English countryside. And as far as I was concerned it was a dead loss. Compared to the beauties of nature which was to be found in Kew Gardens and, to a lesser extent, other London parks, Somerset was a green desert. It was just huge expanses of grass, sometimes hilly and sometimes not, defended from human intrusion by various immense beasts. Some of these were white and woolly and clearly should have been on plates in thin slices drenched in mint sauce but others were tremendous black and brown creatures with horns which no sensible infant would have any communication with. There was a few trees, often set in little groups, but they was nothing like as splendid or as various as the ones in Kew. Every morning I was sent out on a trek compared to which the travels of Stanley in search of Livingstone were like pleasant strolls to reach the school and in the evening the same thing back. I was always escorted on these safaris by one or more of the older children in the family and I used to wonder how they navigated across the trackless wastes.

£ My idea of the Garden of Eden is Piccadilly Circus on a Saturday night

I suppose it was that experience which went a long way towards putting me off the great outdoors for life. The countryside, unless you have business there, should be crossed as swiftly as possible in as magnificent a motor car as you can get your hands on. I would rather steam down Kilburn High Road in a three abreast traffic jam, wedged between a juggernaut and a double-decker, at an average speed of one mile an hour than ramble across the Yorkshire Moors. Which is very handy, given my profession, since of course you can hoof it across the green stuff all day long and find few opportunities for turning over an honest sov.

My exile in the Quantock Hills had lasted three or four lifetimes, and home and the happy streets of Fulham, even if they was getting a bit pitted here and there from the effects of German high explosives, had become but a distant memory, when I got back to the shop in Lower Pendle from school one day and, on entering the little living room at the back, saw a lady standing there.

She was buxom, medium-height and had beautifully coiffeured blonde hair and a lovely smile. I gazed at her for a few moments and noticed that she was holding out her arms to me. And then, my heart gave a great leap and I shouted 'Mum!' and the next moment I had shot across the room like one of the V1s we had yet to experience, and buried my face in her skirts.

In fact, it turned out to be not quite three lifetimes since she had kissed me goodbye on the platform at Paddington and then waved as I was carried off to Somerset, but just over a week. And in that week she had done a lot of thinking. And she had decided that bombs are bad things and kill people. But they only kill a very small proportion of the people beneath them. On the other hand, being separated from your firstborn, when you find it agony to miss a single goodnight kiss, is likely to be a worse health hazard than bombs for you both. And so she had come to take me home. Just in time for the Blitz!

The Blitz didn't do anything like as much damage to Fulham as it did to the poor old East End. But even if my beloved patch had been ground to powder all about me, I still wouldn't have swapped it for the wastes of Somerset.

I was nearly five when the war started. I was nearly eleven when it ended. High time too.

But we weathered the storm and we finally danced in the streets on VE-Day. Well, I didn't actually dance a whole lot because I was too busy touring the street parties in the neighbourhood where they was handing out all the sweets and other goodies that people had been saving up for this event. A nimble nipper like me could stuff himself with more cakes and sweets in that week than he'd had in the whole previous year.

And so at last we had peace. But we was still a

long way from prosperity. There was still rationing. There was still great holes in the town. There was still shabby clothes and shoddy goods. But even an eleven-year-old could see that there was also opportunity. A new world was beginning and I had a pretty clear notion that it could turn out to be just my lobster.

The countryside should whenever possible be crossed in a magnificent motor car

—————CHAPTER THREE—————
THE MAKING OF A TYCOON

T HE OTHER DAY, when I was relaxing in the Winchester over a vodka and slimline, I got to reminiscing with Dave, the owner and barman, about the post-war period and I gave a deep sigh. Dave thereupon asked me why I was exercising the lungs and I replied:

'Just occurred to me, Dave, what a waste of time it was.'

'What was a waste of time, Arthur?' asked the loyal fellow.

'All them years of struggle before I was really established as a successful entrepreneur.'

Dave's blunt, honest face wrinkled up as he asked:

'Successful what was that, Arthur?'

As I often say, this Dave is one of the most devoted friends a man could have, but you is unlikely ever to see him firing off answers to questions put to him by Magnus Magnusson in the black chair of *Mastermind*. Dave's idea of a difficult question is: Who wrote Shakespeare's plays? Other posers which cause him to frown in helpless bafflement are such testing ones as: Is Russia bigger or smaller than Switzerland? Does the sun go round Fulham or is it the other way? And even: What's your home address? But if not actually keeling over under the weight of grey matter packed into his skull, Dave compensates by a kind of sensitivity to the talents of others.

'An entrepreneur, Dave,' I explained slowly because he is not always too agile at catching words of more than one syllable on the wing, 'is

£Dave's idea of a difficult question on Mastermind is: Who wrote Shakespeare's plays?

a very good and successful businessman.'

'Which is exactly what you has always been, Arthur,' Dave exclaimed stoutly. 'I dunno what you're grumbling about. You shot up after the war. People used to talk about the German economic miracle and the Japanese economic miracle. But for my money they was nothing compared to the Daley economic miracle.'

Naturally I smiled appreciatively and noted with satisfaction out of the corner of my eye the goggle-eyed attention of a young street hawker who was one of the latest members of the club and, in my opinion, a symptom of the decline in the Winchester's former high membership standards.

But the fact is that in spite of Dave's stout insistence on my meteoric rise, it really took me quite a long time to scale the heights of economic and social success. It is quite possible, come to think of it, that Dave's mistaken view derives from the fact that he and I were in the same class at school, and, more significantly, we were partners in my very first business venture. It happened like this.

We was out walking in the streets of Fulham after class one spring afternoon when we was about fourteen, lamenting the fact that we hadn't enough money between us to buy either a Tizer or a bag of lemon sherbets when something caught my eye.

Now it will be a big surprise to some of my younger readers to learn that it was quite common to see horse-drawn drays in the streets of London after the Second World War. Straight up, although the war that had just ended had seen terrible scientific marvels like jet aeroplanes, robot bombs and finally atom bombs come into use, there was still a place, in our city streets, for the great plodding cart horses which had pulled Londoners and their goods about since Roman times. This was partly because brewers considered the drays, loaded with barrels

It's not the horse, Dave, it's what's behind it

and pulled by big greys, a good advertisement. But it was also because some firms had found, during the war and the petrol rationing that resulted from it, that they could not lay their hands on enough motor fuel to transport all the things they wanted to transport, and so they had reverted to horses and carts for some of the necessary work. This habit lingered on for a few years after the war until the streets became too congested with motor traffic to permit horses to be used safely any more.

Anyhow, as Dave and I was strolling down Fulham Road gazing hungrily into the windows of sweet shops and discussing, I seem to recall, the mysteries of procreation I stopped suddenly and pointed. I said:

'Hang about, I got an idea.'

'How do you mean, Arthur?' asked young Dave, blinking uncertainly at the two massive greys, harnessed to a flat dray holding empty barrels, that was plodding past on the other side of the street.

'Look at that,' I urged.

'Brewer's dray, Arthur,' protested Dave. 'See them all the time.'

'Not the dray. What's behind it.'

Dave peered but he did not have my lightning nose for an earner and I have to report that he failed to see what I was eagerly gazing at.

'Nothing behind it, Arthur,' he grumbled.

'Isn't there? On the ground? Left there by the horses?'

Dave sniggered.

''Ere, Arthur, you don't mean the horse sh–'.

'The manure. Can't you see it? Lots of manure.'

'I see it all right, Arthur. Disgrace in my opinion. My mum was saying only yesterday the council should be shot because of the state of the streets and –'

'Roses.'

'What?'

'Does your mum grow roses?'

'Nowhere to grow them, Arthur. Not many people got enough space in Fulham. Best Mum can manage is a window-box for a few potatoes.'

'Right, well – what? Your mum grows potatoes in a window-box?'

'Well, she tries. She's Irish, see, and she grew up surrounded by potato fields like they do in Ireland. So she missed them over here and that's why she grows them.'

'Most people grow flowers.'

'Potatoes have flowers. Little white ones. They're quite pretty really.'

'And what are the spuds like? The ones your mum grows?'

'Not much cop, Arthur. Little white marbles – not really worth the boiling.'

'They need manure.'

Dave glanced uneasily at the plodding horses.

'How do you mean?'

'She could grow potatoes like pumpkins. If she had the manure. You know what I was reading, Dave? Just the other day? From the school library?'

'*Beano*?'

'From the library, Dave, not the rubbish bin. I was reading a book called *Making a Start in Business*.'

'Why are we crossing the street, Arthur?'

'Might as well go this way as any other.'

'We're not following them horses, are we?'

'Stop distracting me, Dave. Like I was saying, I was reading how to make a start in business. And you know what the problem facing all budding typhoons is?'

'Isn't a typhoon a kind of hurricane, Arthur?'

'Right. A hurricane of business, which is what I aim to be. But the problem is: how to get your raw material.'

Dave's voice filled with deep reproach.

'You're not suggesting, Arthur, that that horse sh–'

'Without the raw material, you got nothing to sell. And do you know why most budding hurricanes can't get their hands on no raw material?'

'Whoops, there goes another load of raw material, Arthur.'

'Will you listen and learn, Dave? Do you know why it's such a big problem for most blokes like me what wants to be a – a business typhoon? It's because we ain't got no capital.'

'What's capital, Arthur?'

'It's something that people what have got raw material will swap it for. The point is, we haven't got none, have we?'

'I haven't.'

'And nor do I. So now you see what I'm getting at?'

'I gotta go now, Arthur. I promised my –'

''Ang about, Dave! You can go in just one minute. You can go home to your mum and get the shovel and bucket.'

Dave started backing away at this point and so I grabbed his arm and held it in a wrestling lock one of my dad's friends had taught me.

'Owww!' screeched Dave. 'Leggo, Arthur!'

'I will if you'll just listen. What we got here is a source of raw material – pretty much an endless source – and we can get it without needing no capital. It's amazing. I can't imagine why no one's spotted it before. We could easily become the horse sh– the manure kings of Fulham. So if I let you go, Dave, will you nip home and get the shovel and bucket and start collecting the raw material while

I set out to contact potential customers, starting with your ma?',

Dave nodded but then when I released him, he made a break for it. However, I was lighter and faster than him then, just as I am now, and I brought him down about twenty yards along the road just as he was starting to cross it. Funnily enough he came down with his face only a little way from a load of raw material. I think it helped convince him of the beauty of my scheme for after I'd given him another little pep talk as he was lying there he got up and trudged sombrely away to get the shovel and pail.

Well, it was a winner all right. In some ways it was the most successful business venture I ever set up and conducted. In terms of profit margin it was astronomical. The overheads were practically non-existent since we used Dave's mum's bucket and pail. No, that's not quite true because we did have to buy some old paper bags off the grocer to pack the raw material into and then convert it instantly into manure simply by writing 'MANURE' on the bag in black crayon.

Did you ever hear the old song 'Sure Mary this London's a wonderful sight'? Well it's about some very thick Mick from the hills of Ireland who comes to London and is told by some smart aleck for a laugh that the road gangs is digging for gold. He gets a job on one of the gangs but he don't find no gold and he ends up very disillusioned. Now Dave and I, on the contrary, really did find gold in the streets and we didn't even have to dig for it. All Dave had to do was scoop it up. And I could never understand, since I cut him in for a full ten per cent of everything we earned, why he grumbled so much about doing it. After all I never asked him to help out with the really difficult part which was, of course, selling the stuff.

£ Never be reluctant to pay the going rate, or even a bit above it, for top muscle. Apart from anything else it could save you a fortune in medical expenses

Not that, in them days, it was all that difficult. Fulham in the first few years after the war was a very drab kind of place and now that no more bombs were on the way to ruin any decorations anyone put up everyone was interested in beautifying the place. Often I had only to call at a house or flat where I'd seen window-boxes and, with that gift for salesmanship which I must have been born with since I've never done a course in it, hold up a bag of our manure with my cheery grin and say: 'There's five window-boxes full of roses in this bag, Mrs X ['course I didn't actually call her Mrs X but used her real name if I'd been able to find out what it was and otherwise, with simple dignity, 'Madam'], and you can have the whole glorious bouquet of them for a bob.' And usually the colour-starved housewife would cough up without hesitation. Naturally, sometimes I would hit an awkward customer who would lean forwards and sniff and say, 'I wouldn't have that "bokay" [see, it's also a classy French word for a pong] if you gave me a shilling to take it in. So just you remove it from my premises, you young scoundrel, or I'll report you to the health authorities' – but they was a minority and there was never any real trouble shifting the manure.

When I tell you that by the time we'd been in business for a couple of weeks I had taken to strolling about Fulham with a pocket full of sweets just to hand out to some of the street urchins out of pure benevolence and also because they was sometimes useful for fingering possible customers, you will get some idea of the instant success of the enterprise. The only possible items on the debit side were a pong which was beginning to draw adverse comments from some of the teachers and my mum and dad and brothers and sisters, neglect of my homework because of the inevi-

Even the street urchins helped in the success of our venture

table demands of running a thriving commercial operation and Dave's incessant grumbling about his branch of the business. This got so bad that I actually upped his cut to twelve-and-a-half per cent although obviously his duties were purely manual and could have been performed by any of the other kids, who were, by this time, clamorous to be taken into partnership. I only went on using Dave, who was not really a specially useful shovel, out of loyalty and friendship.

Then school broke up for the summer holidays and the business took another leap forwards. You could hardly go for a walk through Fulham in those days without coming upon Dave shovelling away in the middle of the street or plodding after a dray. And before or after seeing him you might easily have also spotted me, bustling in and out of houses and blocks of flats in my best suit, lumbered with no more than a pad and a pencil with which to take orders and a leather wallet for the cash which I insisted on being paid in advance of delivery. Because of the pong factor I had given up actually distributing our manure myself and, to aid my sales pitch, merely held up a bag of brown sugar marked 'MANURE'. Then, when he'd finished his collection duties, I had Dave take round the produce in the evenings using a hand-cart I bought him for nineteen and six from a retired Covent Garden porter.

Nineteen and six was a pretty solid whack of currency in them far-off days and yet I did not even haggle when I bought the cart for Dave. And that gives you some idea of the scale of the operation we was running that happy summer of '48, I think it was, or possibly '49. For myself, I purchased a bicycle to increase my mobility and various little rewards such as a subscription to the *Rover* and several cases of strawberry-flavoured Fizzo, which was the rotgut I favoured in them days.

And then, as has happened before in the history of commerce, I allowed myself to be dazzled by giddy prospects of possible wealth, and diversified to try and increase our turnover but only succeeded in sowing the seeds of rapid decline.

It began one day when I called at a new flat and made my seductive offer to the tall, blonde house-wife what opened the door. She shook her head as soon as she'd grasped what I had on offer.

'No use to me, love. I haven't got a window-box.'

Usually I only called at places that had gardens or boxes as I'd established in advance by eyeballing the outside of the house or from an informant. In this case, lines had got crossed and I had been misinformed. But even before I had begun to turn from the lady's door, that commercial instinct which has been the foundation of all my later achievements, spoke through my mouth:

'S'all right, dear,' I heard myself say. 'We can supply those too.'

She looked doubtful.

'They're expensive.'

'Not ours ain't. Very reasonable. Less than you pay in the shops –'

'Well –'

'Tell you what, I'll bring one round later. Just to show you. And – and –'

And now, I think the unbiased reader will agree, sheer genius made its presence felt.

'And you'll want it planted, won't you?'

'Planted?'

'With plants and flowers. I could do a nice selection for you. Just give me the word and I'll bring it round later – or –' I concluded grandly, 'get my man to.'

'But what if I don't like it?'

'You don't have to take it, dear. Always a queue waiting for our boxes. No trouble shifting it elsewhere.'

Note that 'dear'. You might think this would be regarded as cheeky by a grown-up housewife but again my commercial instincts, in this case tending in the direction of psychology, were sound. I was about fourteen and looked, if anything, young for my age, say twelve or thirteen. I needed something – a manner, a form of address, a style – to give me a façade of maturity. That's why I often called busty housewives 'dear'. And they loved it.

'All right then,' she said. 'See you later.'

And with a smile and a shrug, she shut her kitchen door.

I ran, perhaps I even skipped, down to the river where the Maisie Plant Nursery was located in them days. This was nothing like the great garden centres which have colonised so much of England in recent years. More of a greenhouse with a little office next to it. But it did do window-boxes and I knew with icy clarity how to get what I wanted.

'How much for a window-box planted with nice flowering plants?' I asked the lone girl potting seedlings.

She glanced up and looked a bit surprised at my youth. But she took me seriously.

'One pound, seventeen and six for one like that one over there,' she said, pointing to a nicely planted trough.

It seemed a tremendous sum to me in them days and I felt like a Titan of the exchange dealing in such figures. It was nevertheless with the icy calm of the born entrepreneur that I continued quictly:

'Now go and ask your dad – and tell him to give it some thought because it could turn out to be a very big deal for both of us – how much discount he'd give me if I took twenty of these a week.'

She cocked her head a little to suggest she thought I might be taking the mickey. But my calm and confident manner convinced her I was genuine. She said:

'Hang on a sec –'

And she tripped away to consult her green-fingered father. When she came back, five or six minutes later, she said:

'You could have them for twenty-five bob each.'

Preserving my outer calm, although exploding inwardly with delight at the realisation that I was heading for riches, I said, with a big, friendly smile:

'Done. Tell your dad he'll never regret it,' and I turned and strode importantly away.

For the next three weeks, Dave and I practically coined money. We consumed all the sweets and Fizzo we could hoist on board and we thought nothing of taking girls on outings to cinemas and fun-fairs. We even made a day trip on the river in the company of two very comely young ladies from the form ahead of us. Although well known for their picky attitude to male escorts, they suggested to Dave and me, as we were gliding under Tower Bridge, stuffing ourselves on fish and chips, that we should all go steady. Sadly they proved fickle when our fortunes changed, as I shall have to relate in due course, but for three whole weeks our idyll continued and we basked continually in financial sunshine. In many cases, we sold a package deal of a planted box and two sacks of manure for thirty-five bob making a princely ten shillings on the call. We took out post office savings accounts and we was probably two of the richest schoolboys in South London – definitely front-runners in the juvenile plutocratic set.

And then the funny things began to happen.

I came out of a house with an order for three window-boxes and some manure one afternoon and stopped dead at the gate. My eyes narrowed and a slight frown clouded my features which, in them days, normally wore a look of success and prosperity. My anxiety was caused by what I was looking at on the other side of the road. It was a boy leaning against a lamppost. Nothing specially alarming about that, you may think, but you would be wrong. In the first place, this was one of the most menacing-looking boys I had ever seen. He was about my age but looked leaner and meaner. His clothes consisted of a large number of holes held together by rags. Some time in the past his outfit had probably been a suit but it had clearly fallen on, and then passed, evil days and by the time it had descended to its present occupant it was nothing that would interest a scarecrow. I eyeballed him long enough to spot that he was also wearing an ancient hat pulled low over his minces, had a toe protruding from a convenient hole in one shoe and, above all, possessed two sharp ferrety little eyes. But it was not his appearance alone which caused me to gasp slightly and become aware of something that felt like a troupe of performing spiders doing Cossack dances on the top of my scalp. It was the fact that I had spied this very same boy, engaged in exactly the same surveillance operation, only the day before in a different part of the manor. I had acquired the first of what, for one reason or another, has proved to be a long succession of tails.

For a moment I debated with myself the wisdom of crossing the road and asking him if he was following me. But uncertainty as to how I should proceed with the conversation if he replied in the affirmative deterred me and I slipped through the gate and then hastened away down the street, very conscious of those two ferrety eyes boring into my back.

As I made my way to the bombsite where I had arranged to meet Dave, I mulled it over. But the only thing that seemed clear to me was that it boded no good. Even if the ferrety-eyed kid was just a street nut I knew it wouldn't be long before I began to find his observation of me intolerable. I considered telling Dave what was going on to see if he had any ideas as to what to do about it but I refrained, chiefly because I had never known Dave to have an idea about anything. So I kept shtum and for several days it seemed that this had been the best policy. Although I now paused habitually on my rounds and glanced stealthily about there was no more appearances by the ferrety-eyed bloke and I began to feel the threat had passed. How wrong can you be? On the fourth day from my last sighting I went to meet Dave as usual and found him sobbing. This was uncharacteristic since, although not a front runner in the IQ stakes, Dave has always displayed a dogged courage. But I could see from a distance that he was surprisingly in tears, sitting on a crate in the bombsite and, as I got nearer, I perceived sufficient cause for his distress. He was liberally smeared with raw material. In fact, if he had dived head-first into a vat of our product he could not have had a thicker layer of – of manure on him.

'What's happened to you?' I asked aghast, picking up an old rusty rake-head and trying to dislodge some of the thicker deposits from Dave's clothing.

'Big bloke, Arthur,' sobbed Dave, 'just come up to me as I was scooping, tripped me up and then rolled me about in it.'

'Why? What did he do that for?'

'Dunno. He didn't say nothing. Just rolled me

about in it. How can I go home? My mum will go berserk.'

'Yeah well – go what?' I asked, astonished at hearing what sounded like a very classy word from Dave's lips.

'Berserk. It means – you know – wild, angry.'

'We got to get you cleaned up.'

'I wish to tender my resignation.'

'What?'

'I've had enough. The material's getting too raw for me, Arthur. I've got a few bob in the post office now and I want to quit and seek my fortune elsewhere.'

I couldn't believe my ears.

'Oh, that's nice, isn't it? You've made your pile and now you want out. There's gratitude. I cut you in on the most grandiose profit-making

Dave and I riding the crest of the manure wave

scheme ever devised by a schoolboy and you want to leave me in the lurch!'

'It's just that –'

'It's just that you're very naturally upset because of your ruined clothes. Well, I'll tell you what, I'll let you have a nice whistle and flute of my own – my second best.'

'That's good of you, Arthur, but –'

'At a very reasonable price too. But, come on, we'll get you presentable and then nip into Minsky's [a local milkbar] and hold a council of war.'

'Well, I dunno, Arthur –'

But the devoted fellow as usual allowed me to take charge and we did what I had proposed. At Minsky's we did not stint ourselves in raspberry milkshakes and jam tarts although my pleasure in them was reduced by the fact that Dave, although thoroughly bathed and now clad in completely new clothing, still exuded a pong like a badly ventilated stable.

'What's it all about, Arthur?' asked Dave after I had told him about the ferrety-eyed spy.

'I think that's what we is going to find out quite soon, Dave, and whatever it turns out to be it's got to be bad news. So the question is: How do we get ready to meet the threat? And the answer, I think, has to be: Rodney Travers.'

Dave frowned, trying to make the connection, a task he is never specially good at.

'Rodney Travers is that big gorilla in the sixth form, isn't he, Arthur?'

'No. Rodney Travers is our new minder.'

'What's a minder, Arthur?'

'It sometimes happens, Dave, that honest businessmen like us is troubled by the hooligan element –'

'What's that?'

'I'm not exactly sure, Dave, but I suspect it's something very like these two young thugs that is causing us grief. So, like grown-up honest business-men what is troubled by the hooligan element, we must hire a minder.'

'What does the minder do?'

'Whatever needs to be done. If these two come back – as I have no doubt they will – our minder will make them sorry they did and ensure that they never bother us no more.'

Dave did not reply and when I glanced up over my straw I saw that there was something like a worried crease on his boyish brow.

'Something wrong with that scheme, Dave?' I asked gently.

'Dunno, Arthur. The one what rolled me about – pretty tough nut was my impression.'

'Was he bigger than Rodney Travers?'

'Well no, but –'

'Rodney is the school weightlifting, boxing, wrestling, swimming and ping-pong champion. Should be a match for street toughs, shouldn't he?'

'S'pose so, Arthur.'

'Come on, have another milkshake to put a bit of fight back into you and then we'll go and hire Rodney.'

Recognise the name? Rodney Travers? Quite probably you do because he was, before his tragi-cally early death five or six years ago, Member of Parliament in the Labour interest for Bridlington-on-Sea. Straight up. Not only brawn but brains had Rodney, and, along with one other whom modesty forbids me to name, was amongst the most cel-ebrated alumni of Morgan's Road School.

So we offered Rodney a prince's ransom, in schoolboy terms, for his services, i.e. a pound note, a half-full pint-sized bottle of strawberry

Fizzo, a pound of mixed chocolate seconds and
the promise of a further quid in cash if, a month
after whatever devastation he wreaked upon them,
the two unsavoury characters had still not returned
to bother us. He jumped at it with a cry of:

'Whizzo! What fun. I'm jolly grateful to you
chaps for this exciting opportunity. Let's get started.
Arthur, you're tophole in my book from now on.'

He always talked like that, did Rodney Travers
and that was another bond between us. He was
at the Morgan's Road school because, like mine
years before, his family had unexpectedly lost all
their money and so he had been unable to go to
Eton or Rugby which was where the males of his
family usually went. He was keen as mustard and
it was his idea to set up an ambush.

Dave had received the brunt of the enemy
attack and so, although he grumbled a bit about
it, Rodney and I chose him to be the decoy. He
was stationed in a quiet street, filling buckets with
raw material in the usual way, while Rodney and
I kept him under observation from a concealed
place. This was so we could spring out and save
him when the enemy turned up. And everything
went exactly according to plan.

Dave was scooping up the raw material from
a rich seam that he had found on Domney Close
which ran down from the High Street to the
brewery stables, and Rodney and I were peeping
through knot-holes in a fence round a bombsite
when them two hooligan elements appeared at the
top of the street and slouched down to where Dave
was working. I recognised one of them immediately
as the element which had been spying on me, and
the other was a broad bloke, not so tall as Rodney,
but very powerful looking. They began the encounter without any ceremony by kicking Dave's bucket
over. This was done by the smaller, and then the

bigger one reached down and tugged Dave to his feet. He drew back his fist and then paused and looked in our direction. This was because Rodney and I, having stepped out from behind the concealing fence, were now charging towards the group, shouting and yelling and making a terrific hullabaloo.

'Leave him alone!' I shouted.

'Stop that, you rotters!' thundered Rodney.

And then we came up to them. And after that there was a short pause for everyone to size everyone else up. It was then that I noticed that the bigger of the two hooligan elements, whom I was seeing now for the first time, did give an impressive sense of raw power. He was not quite as tall as Rodney but his shoulders stuck out like the prows of two destroyers. Still, I comforted myself, it was probably mainly padding which was fashionable in them days and worn by the Teddy Boys. His face was a bit square but did not have the foxy, slightly evil cast of the other's.

'Right,' I said firmly. 'You two has been harassing us. I want to know why.'

'It's pairfectly simple,' said the smaller of the two and somehow it gave me a shock to hear that he had a broad Scotch accent. 'We've decided to take over your business. So if you two just clear off, there'll be no more trouble.'

This was effrontery indeed. I was so surprised that for a moment I just gawped at the little ferret.

'Let's get this straight,' I said finally. 'You is proposing that Dave and I, who has built up this thriving little business empire from scratch by our honest toil –'

At this point Dave made a faint sound as if he was not completely sure I was putting things accurately but then fell silent again. I continued:

'You really think we're just gonna hand it all over to you two?'

'Aye,' said the small one crisply.

'Why should we?'

'Because if you don't, we'll pound you into haggis, won't we, Wullie?' he appealed to his larger companion in crime.

'Aye,' confirmed the other simply.

The pink petunia hat gone, I think it is fair to say that it was with a kind of sublime sang-froid that I turned to Rodney and murmured:

'I think these two is in need of a spanking, Rodney.'

'As you say, Arthur,' agreed our new minder and without further ado he pushed out a nice firm right jab to the big one's jaw. He didn't telegraph the punch or nothing. But oddly enough it never connected. And after that things rapidly got very exciting but also confusing. The big one, who must have sideslipped Rodney's punch, reached out an arm like the boom of a hydraulic ram, seized Rodney's wrist and then, with a delicate-seeming little flick, caused Rodney to spin half round and assume a squatting posture. After that, he frog-marched Rodney round and round in circles, kicking him smartly on the Khyber at every step. Rodney gave a yell as the boot first connected, and then continued yelling rhythmically, like a novelty clock, as he received regular thumps on his backside.

After watching this surprising and impressive spectacle for a while, my concentration was disturbed by a curious sound and, turning to find out its cause, I was distressed to see that Dave had decided to lie down on his back in the road with the smaller of the two elements kneeling on his chest and twisting his nose. Dave's attempts, with his nose out of action, to express suitable

resentment at this process had been responsible
for the distressing stifled squeal that had caught
my attention. For a few moments I contented
myself with glancing back and forth, in mingled
astonishment and, I have to confess, admiration
from one to the other of the two unequal pairs.
What was taking place was not, of course, fighting, but simple chastisement. Then a disturbing
consideration occurred to me. Sooner or later, it
seemed probable, one of the two Scotch bruisers
would exhaust the fun-potential of their present
victims and look about for further sport. And there
didn't seem anyone in the neighbourhood capable

*A new world was
dawning and even
a schoolboy could
smell opportunity*

of providing it other than yours truly. To perceive the danger was, for my quick brain, virtually the same as averting it. Stealthily, and trying not to draw any unseemly attention to myself, I backed slowly away from the scene of punishment and when I'd got to what seemed a reasonable distance I turned and ran like hell for home.

Strangely enough, when I met the other two later in the day, neither of them seemed disposed to offer me much in the way of reproach for my desertion. Rodney at first maintained a little peevishly that if I'd caused a diversion by attacking the big bully, we might together have made a fight of it. But by and large, both Rodney and Dave recognised that the three of us had been hopelessly outnumbered by the two of them and that discretion had certainly, on that occasion, been the better part of valour.

And that turned out to be the end of the great manure cartel which was, as I have said, not only my first business venture but one which, in many ways, can be seen as a model for all my later commercial triumphs. What, you are surprised that we chucked in the towel so readily? Yeah, well – I knew we could have gone out searching for a heftier minder than poor, gentleman-league Rodney had proved to be. But the fact was that both Dave and I was beginning to feel that we had had enough of the manure trade. The sheer buccaneering thrill of it (without which business is just as humdrum as what 'er indoors does all day) had worn off. Moreover, it was nearly term time again and we both realised that our scholastic careers would be on the line, upsetting our parents, if we went on devoting as much time as we had been doing to commerce. Dave also, and very forcibly, expressed the view that he would be happy never again to see the rear-end of a horse. And so we pulled out and left the two Jock tearaways a clear field. And we sometimes saw them about the manor, just as we had been, lugging the bags and boxes about to different houses and flats but we didn't see them for long. Because, you see, there was another reason why we had left the field to the enemy with so little fight.

Dave's dad, who worked for the brewery, had let fall at the family dinner table one evening that the brewery was closing down its stables and converting to motor transport. There were, as I have said, other horse-drawn vehicles, like milk floats, on the streets in them days but our staple source of raw material had been the great brewery greys which had discharged such golden treasure onto the streets. Within a month of the hooligan's element's victory, the greys had vanished and a week or two later those Glasgow gangsters had disappeared too and I never did find out what had become of them.

So what did it teach me, the whole episode? How to sell, the value of a monopoly, the importance of a good discount, the necessity to pay fair wages and many, many more things. But if I was to name the one lesson which I thoroughly absorbed and which has been instrumental in guiding my triumphant business career ever since it is this: always make sure you've got a top-of-the-league minder. You're not looking for trouble but if it comes along, you've got to be able to dish out more than you receive. So economise on your raw material like we did. Keep your overheads as low as possible just like we did. Don't throw your money around in milk bars or, in later life, gambling hells and here we lapsed a little sometimes. But above all, never be reluctant to pay the going rate, or even a bit above it, for top muscle. Apart from anything else it could save you a fortune in medical expenses.

CHAPTER FOUR

OUR DALEY BREAD

IT TOOK ME MORE THAN fifteen years to find the perfect minder and, in this chapter, I'm going to tell you how it came about. But, you are probably wondering, what happened to me in that long stretch of time? And the answer is: more of the same. It was really a case of making steady progress towards success and achievement.

After my early triumph in the manure business, I settled down to my studies again and finally left school with dozens of both O- and A-levels. And then I started my business career proper. Now many young men would have opted for the security of a job. They would have taken employment with some company to gain experience before setting up on their own. But that was not for me. I was always a loner, supremely confident of my own ability and happier with a crust that I'd earned by my own efforts than a plate of fish and chips in the company canteen. Not that crusts ever figured very much in my diet. It's true I had a few somewhat difficult years right at first when more money seemed to flow out of my bank account than flowed in. But I continued to live at home and Mum saw to it that I never lacked for three square meals a day. My only recreation was a glass of lager now and then down at the Conservative Club where I went chiefly to make contacts. And slowly my dedication and talent for innovation began to pay off.

I invented, for example, the only floating second-hand car lot in the country. At that time London was still scarred with bombsites from the war. The big development booms of the sixties

I was always a loner, happier with a crust that I'd earned by my own efforts than a plate of fish and chips in the company canteen

had not started and they was mainly weed-clogged expanses covered in the ruins of buildings.

I hit on the idea of starting Daley's Floating Car Mart. I hired a vacant lot at a peppercorn rent, smoothed it up a bit, spread it with top-class used cars and, when the site was wanted for development, simply moved the whole outfit to a new bombsite. In this way, I kept overheads to practically nothing and soon I found my bank account was in the black.

What with this and other exciting business ventures, I had become, by my mid-twenties, perhaps the most dynamic young entrepreneur in Fulham.

Picture me then at this time, ensconced in my split-level fab. lux. pent. mais. overlooking the river at the bottom of Walmer Street. There in the early sixties, I lived the life every virile, talented young Londoner yearned for. And what kind of life was that? One long, lovely, lusty party is what it was. Every night to some new venue for dinner and dancing. Every night a different companion. Looking back from the present post-Thatcherite gloom it seems the whole of Fulham was one great glittering playground.

Floating through the streets were girls dressed in tiny skirts and see-through blouses. It was like living on the stage of the Folies Bergère. There was an atmosphere of carnival, of revelry. It was no unlikely scene if cars pulled up beside you filled with laughing young things who'd drag you in and haul you off to a party. You had to be a little careful because sometimes thieves took advantage of this cordial custom and just turned you over and dumped you out into the gutter. This happened to friends of mine a few times but in my own case I was such a well-known Fulham figure that it would have been unthinkable. So the invitations just went on piling up on my Adam mantelpiece. My only

I became the most dynamic young entrepreneur in London

problem each evening was deciding which one to accept.

But the thing which makes a good party is the fact that it has to end. A party which goes on too long just becomes a seedy gathering of bored people who need more and more stimulation to get fewer and fewer kicks. For me the party began to end as I approached thirty. And providentially it was then that I first made the acquaintance of the gracious lady who, after a proper courtship lasting a year and half, consented to become my wife.

Now nothing would have given me greater delight than to have devoted a chapter entirely to singing 'er praises. But when I suggested this to 'er, she said simply, 'I will not have it, Arthur.'

'Why not, my love?' I asked, astonished.

'You know I am a very private person. I would be completely mortified to think that everyone knew all our little secrets.'

Thinking it over, I saw that 'er had a point. In any case I would never dream of writing, or indeed doing anything else, that she had taken objection to. Moreover, I am confident that all my readers will remember that standing behind every successful man like myself is a woman with a dirty great rolling pin – ha! ha! nuff said.

I take up the tale again when we had been happily married for about five years, settled in a nice detached house in Sempleton Drive and produced two pre-school kiddies whom we both doted on. But what I did not yet have was a reliable and efficient minder.

Anyway one night I was cruising down the English Channel in my superb 18-cylinder Jaguar saloon with electric everything and a flush toilet. In the back was stowed bales of priceless silks, kegs of rum and brandy, cases of spices and chests of jewels which included rubies the size of pigeons' eggs and diamonds that sparkled like the evening star. I intended to berth in Huggett Wharf, Fulham, the following morning in order to offload the cargo. This would then be picked up and carted away in team-drawn covered wagons led by Wild Bill Hickock smoking one of the new-fangled 'cigar-eets'. As payment he would hand over to me a stack of gold ingots as high as St Paul's Cathedral and also make me a hereditary chief of the Mohicans. But what was this? From behind came the unmistakable zoot ZooT ZOOT! of a destroyer's superchargers and, glancing round, I saw the knife-edged prow of the craft coming up over the horizon at about five-hundred miles per hour. I stepped on the accelerator and my Jag shot forwards obediently but moments later I heard a voice calling:

My superb 18-cylinder Jaguar saloon with a flush toilet

'Arthur Daley? Arthur Daley? Wake up, Arthur. Arthur, wake up, do you hear?'

At this point my Jaguar began to rock violently as if a sudden hurricane had sprung up and, a moment later, as the car began to sink, I opened my eyes to find that 'er indoors was shaking me violently.

'Wake up, Arthur,' 'er ordered once more. 'There's someone at the door.'

'Oh Gawd!' I exclaimed with a deep sigh. 'Not Dandy Dick again. That's the second time this week.'

'Go down, dear. Before he busts in the front door,' 'er urged.

"E does and 'e'll get a hefty bill for damages,' I promised sternly, trying to recall if I'd paid VAT on the pigeon's egg rubies or not. Then, grumbling and sighing, I rose, donned my rainbow-pattern shot silk dressing-gown and shuffled off down the hall and then the stairs towards the front door from which the waves of clamour got louder and louder.

'Hang about!' I called as I got near it. 'Give us time to hide the swag.'

Then I pulled the door open to reveal, as I'd expected, the high-browed, bespectacled face of young Detective-Sergeant Richard Swann-Haverstock of the Fulham CID. He smiled brightly.

'Hello, Arthur,' he greeted me. 'Sorry to interrupt your beauty sleep. What a glorious dressing-gown. Woolworths or Marks and Sparks?'

'I'll have you know –' I began indignantly, but then pulled myself up. Playing into his hands, wasn't it?

'Litter bin outside the cop shop, actually. Might be your chief super's cast-off. What can I do for you, Sergeant Swann-Haverstock, as if I didn't know?'

'We just thought we might have a look round, Arthur,' said the well-spoken peeler who, I had been told, held a degree in philosophy from Oxford University. 'Come on, Pigsby,' he urged his lethargic DC, a plump Londoner who obviously detested his superior but lacked the verbal dexterity to even make the odd snide remark.

They both moved forwards but I held up a restraining hand:

'Uh uh, let's preserve the formalities,' I cautioned. 'I assume you've got one?'

'Arthur,' grinned the upper-crust bogy. 'You

didn't think we were trying it on, did you? Here it is, all beautifully signed by His Honour Sir John Aubrey.'

And he held up the search warrant for me to inspect.

'Seems to be in order,' I conceded. 'Right, where do you want to search first? Under the bed? I believe there's a very fine antique porcelain item there which you could either impound or empty.'

'Let's not get too cheeky too soon, shall we, Arthur?' suggested Swann-Haverstock cheerfully. Well, why wouldn't he be cheerful? After slumming about on the beat and in the junior ranks of the CID for a couple of years he'd then shoot to the top like a New York lift. In under ten years he'd be an assistant commissioner, taking fat bribes from half of Soho.

'I suggest we start at the top and work down,' he opined.

He'd soon be an assistant commissioner, taking bribes from half of Soho

'You're not going to wake the kids again, are you? I mean if you want to eviscerate their teddy bears in your search for pigeon's egg rubies, you'll find all the toys in the hall cupboard. But do let the little perishers sleep. I give you my word there's no contraband in their room.'

'I certainly have no wish to disturb innocent children, Arthur,' affirmed Swann-Haverstock. 'So let's hope we find – well – *them* before we reach the nursery.'

'Them? And what exactly would "them" be, Sergeant?'

'Oh, just some small items of considerable value.'

'Pigeon's egg rubies?'

'Not quite, Arthur, but precious enough. I have every reason to believe that *they* will be found somewhere on the premises.'

'Your usual reliable informant?' I could not

resist taunting him, since he had found nothing of consequence on his last two after-midnight raids on the besieged castle which was what my Englishman's home had recently become. But he ignored the taunt.

'I hope you won't mind, Arthur,' he said with a well-bred leer in his voice, 'if my colleague keeps your lovely wife company while you and I are in the attic? We can't have her popping out of bed the minute we're out of sight to chuck things out of the window, can we?'

'Immoral!' I grumbled. 'I could get you pilloried in the *Fulham Gazette* for your licentious tactics.'

'But would it be wise, Arthur, since Pigsby has put in time with your wife on previous occasions without any complaint from you.'

I sighed. 'All right. The attic then.'

So we plodded in a small procession up the stairs. When we reached the door to my bedroom I opened it to see 'er sitting up, modestly wrapped in a negligée.

'Usual drill, I fear, my love,' I explained sadly. 'Cruel and unusual punishments was supposed to have gone out with Oliver Cromwell but I fear you've drawn Pigsby again. Incidentally, if he's not the perfect gentleman in word and deed, just scream and I'll come running.'

'Er nodded in resignation and took up *The Care of House Plants* which was her current bedside book. Pigsby stationed himself unhappily by the door and folded his arms to try and look aloof and official. And I continued on up the attic stairs. At the top I flung open the door and switched on the light.

'Satisfied?' I asked caustically. 'It's exactly as it was last Thursday when you last paid us a visit.'

I thereupon switched off the light again and prepared to pull the door shut. But 'Havers' firmly planted his foot in the gap.

'Really, Arthur, that was a bit lacking in finesse even for you.'

'You don't mean you wants to prowl about again? Look, Sergeant, how's this for an idea? You could rent our attic. I'll get 'er to make it nice and cosy and –'

'Less lip, Arthur. Open the door,' ordered Havers, beginning to show signs of irritation.

I did as he had instructed me, murmuring:

'Untouched since you was last here. Straight up.'

I seated myself on a large packing case. Just as I'd planned he would, he immediately pointed at it and barked:

'What's in there?'

'Curling tongs. Same ones as last Thursday.'

'Off.'

Sighing, I shifted myself from my perch. Old Havers opened the case and rummaged about amongst dozens of curling tongs for some little time. Finally and a little sheepishly he growled:

'Right.'

'Wrong. It's not right. It's harassment, that's what it is. You can see that nothing's changed.'

'No, I can't, Arthur. All I have seen so far is that this packing case still contains curling irons. But there are twenty or thirty other containers in this room and I intend to examine them all.'

He thereupon started ripping and tearing and prising and peering and shuffling and upsetting and spilling and ferreting and –

'Got it!' I exclaimed. 'It's a needle you're looking for, isn't it? I thought even the Old Bill knew you have to have a haystack to find one of those in. So why don't we call it a day, Sergeant?'

'Don't provoke me, Arthur. I have very polished manners but I am a cop. And I respond to aggro not as an Oxford philosopher but as a cop.'

'Point taken, Sergeant,' I murmured soothingly. 'But you've inspected it all now. Opened
everything. Whatever it is you hoped to find, the
truth of the matter is that you've had a duff tip.
Isn't that so?'

'Well no, Arthur, it's not,' purred Sergeant
Swann-Haverstock in a voice that had suddenly
become unpleasantly silky. 'You see I haven't yet
examined – wait for it – that!'

And he shot out a menacing finger and pointed
to a small parcel, hardly bigger than a detergent
carton, which was nestling inconspicuously in an
angle of the rafters.

I frowned.

'That? No interest to you, Sergeant. All that
contains is – er – well, let's see – it's only –'

'Get it down, Arthur.'

'Oh, have a heart, Sergeant. We'll be up all
night. Very upsetting for 'er downstairs, not to
mention Pigsby I shouldn't wonder and –'

'Arthur, down.'

'If you insist, Sergeant. However, I've just
recalled that I haven't yet stumped up my annual
contribution to the police orphans and widows
benevolent fund. The very moment we get back
downstairs I intend to write out a very meaty
cheque which you –'

I fell silent. This was because Havers, apparently tired of waiting, had pulled over an old
backless chair and, mounting on it a trifle pre-
cariously, had managed to reach the small brown-
paper-wrapped parcel I had earlier put up there. I
watched with a somewhat troubled expression as,
back at ground level, he held the parcel close to
his right ear and shook it slightly. It rattled as if
containing small, loose objects. He grinned.

'Promising, Arthur. Very promising,' he said

happily.

'Mr Swann-Haverstock,' I said humbly, knowing how gratified detective-sergeants are to be called Mr just as if they were people. 'You're barking up the wrong –'

'What's in this box?' he snapped.

'Boxes,' I muttered.

'How do you mean "boxes"?'

'I mean there's boxes in the box.'

'But what's rattling in the box?'

'It must be the boxes.'

£ Standing behind every successful man like myself is a woman with a dirty great rolling pin

'Arthur, the prison gates yawn for the impenitent sinner – as the poet said or should have done if he didn't. Now lend me your ears. What do you make of this sound?' He shook the box once more. 'Would you say it was more suggestive of the noise made by boxes or – wait for it – industrial diamonds?'

I blinked at him in well-simulated amazement.

'Industrial – no, 'ang about, Mr Swann-Haverstock. Even if I was the habitual felon you mistake me for, that kind of thing would be right outside my league. I wouldn't recognise an industrial diamond if it stopped me in the street and offered to sell me three gross of slightly shop-soiled curling tongs at well under the odds.'

'So what's rattling, Arthur?'

'No idea. There's boxes in the box, I know that. And quite possibly there's also a novelty. That's right, there's very likely to be a novelty inside the boxes in the box. So it must be the novelty that's rattling.'

'I'll have a look.'

'Now just a sec, Mr Swann-Haverstock,' I exclaimed urgently. 'Before you start ripping and –'

But I again fell silent. He had already ripped away most of the brown wrapping paper which, when it came away completely a moment later, revealed a cardboard box that looked a bit like a large shoe box.

'Now you say there are boxes in this box, do you, Arthur?' purred Havers with a very nasty sneer.

'It's what I was told when ordering.'

'Let's just confirm that,' boomed Havers and, with a theatrical flourish, he whipped off the lid.

We both peered down at the contents. It seemed to be little plastic cubes of various colours arranged in three rows.

'Hm,' said Havers, a little taken aback. 'All right, Arthur, round one to you. It seems there are indeed boxes in the box. But the big question is: what's inside the boxes in the box?'

'More boxes,' I suggested.

'Arthur!' growled Havers warningly.

He prised out a little box and it proved to be a cube with one side missing which contained another cube with one side missing.

'I believed they is called Chinese Boxes, Mr Swann-Haverstock,' I opined.

'I know that, Arthur. But there's something that rattles in the smallest box in the middle.'

He thereupon set about finding out what it was that rattled. This proved quite a challenge, for the plastic boxes was very well made and there was eleven of them to be opened and each of those was difficult because the set fitted so tightly together. But finally, triumphantly, Havers held in his hand a tiny orange-coloured box, just a little larger than a thimble.

'Still rattles, Arthur,' he said eagerly, demonstrating the fact.

'But you can see, Mr Swann-Haverstock, it's an intact cube, not a five-sided cube like the others. It can't be opened.'

'Oh dear,' grumbled Havers as if in considerable distress. 'Do you mean we've come all this way for nothing?'

'Looks like it,' I said.

He shook his head purposefully.

'No, I'm not beaten yet. After all diamonds are very hard, aren't they?'

And before I could make a move to stop him he had dropped the tiny box onto the floor and stamped on it with his heel. Then he bent down and scooped up the resulting little heap of plastic fragments, held it up to his face and poked about in it with his free forefinger, gazing hard. To his obvious astonishment something gazed back. He gave a slight gasp and then picked out of his left palm an eerily well-made glass eye. It had cost me quite a lot to have the whole box of tricks made to my specifications but it was all worth it for that moment. Swann-Haverstock and the glass eye glowered at each other. Then he flung the object away with an exclamation of the kind that I presume does not echo about amongst the quads and halls of Oxford, and exclaimed:

'Damn you, Arthur. I think you've set me up. Do all the boxes end in glass eyes?'

'Now that you mention it, I believe they do. Oh well, win a few, lose a few, eh, Mr Swann-Haverstock?'

He offered me a bleak smile.

'I'll get the rest opened down at the station,' he said grimly.

'Hope you take this in the right spirit, Mr Swann-Haverstock, but don't you think you should get yourself a new snout?'

But a little later, as I closed the door after the two detectives I suddenly perceived that the whole operation had been stupid. The second rule of life for all those whose business activities sometimes bring them into unfriendly contact with the police is: Don't make waves. (The first is, of course: Don't get caught.) What is the point of winding up the Old Bill unless there's something of value, beyond sheer entertainment, to be gained from it? I had kidded myself that I was acting rationally. I had figured that Havers must be getting near the end of his credit down at the nick as regards 'the Arthur Daley investigation' since, after six months of harassing me he had not turned up a single piece of evidence that would stand up in court. So I had reasoned that if I could set up something time-consuming and humiliating like the present 'box of tricks' and make sure the chief super got to hear about it then Havers might receive a summons to his office and hear something like: 'Sergeant, you've had your chance to bring Arthur Daley to book. Has it occurred to you that there may be nothing whatever to book? So perhaps you'd now gratify me by laying off this blameless citizen and buckling down to some real police work or I'll have you back on the streets without your stripes before you can say, "high flyer".'

But I think that really I knew all along that I was chiefly doing it for a laugh. You see, the fact has to be faced: I was just then at a pretty low ebb in my career. Although he had not found anything dodgy on his many raids on my home, Havers had in fact succeeded in stifling my business activities. No one wants to trade with someone that's got a bogy practically sitting on his shoulder. Then again because of the regular presence of Havers in my attic, which was where I kept my trade goods, I had been unable to stock certain sensitive lines which, while perfectly reputable and in great demand, did sometimes generate the interests of the courts. So, chiefly because of Havers I was in the grip of a severe cash-flow problem and could just about be said to have reached the nadir of my business career. I had even been sadly considering selling the family home in order to acquire trading capital.

So I knew really that pulling the rug out from under Havers had been little more than a *jeu d'esprit*, a gallows joke, a last frolic, rather than a considered plan to escape persecution by the rozzers. And even as I watched a manifestly raging and vindictive Swann-Haverstock and a quietly mutinous Pigsby roll away in their toytown Ford Escort I felt apprehension about the future.

That very evening 'er and I had a long heart-to-heart and finally decided that our best plan, especially for the kids, would be to uproot and seek our fortunes in the Antipodes. True, the thought of spending the rest of my days upside down, and even more of being sundered from my beloved Fulham, weighed on me like a massive dud cheque. But what was the alternative? An office job? No, it would be the end of me. Without the freedom to wheel and deal, to seek my fortune by my own initiative, I would wither like the rose before the frost. I was a free spirit, a self-made entrepreneur, not an office lackey. So Australia here we come.

It was none the less with leaden heart that I sallied forth the next morning to make enquiries at the town hall about assisted passages to the land of the koala and the kangaroo. As I rolled down Brecknock Street in my Jaguar saloon, I gazed hungrily about at the sights of my native parish. There was the convent church. There was the off-licence where you could get discount Russian vodka. This was a real bargain as I knew because I supplied it. The stuff was made by two Fulham Russians in their basement flat according to a formula which their refugee ancestors had brought over from the Ukraine or the Migraine or one of them bits of Mother Russia. Just over there was the drinking

fountain with the horse-trough. And just beyond
it was a superb lock-up for sale which –

A WHAT!?!

The Jaguar screeched to a halt in a cloud of
brake lining smoke. A lock-up! I'd been searching
for one for what seemed like years without success.
Indeed I'd been looking for the right lock-up from
the start of my financial career. I'd had lock-ups,
of course, and some of them had been moderately
satisfactory but a lock-up which possessed all the
qualities that I really needed had so far eluded me.
What were these qualities? In the first place it had
to be the right distance from home. It mustn't be
so near that 'er indoors, on her not infrequent
expeditions out of doors, would be able to drop in
at any moment either with requests for my services
or simply to poke about and ask awkward questions
about some of the items she might find there.

Perhaps I should at this point explain that 'er –
while the perfect helpmeet for a dedicated tycoon
– was a little naive in her attitude to commercial
matters. She never did understand that it is sometimes necessary to use unorthodox and unofficial
channels in the procurement and distribution of the
range of goods dealt with by an organisation such
as Daley Enterprises. I had once unwisely mentioned that I was leaving the house at two a.m. to
receive a consignment of Swedish car parts which
would be arriving at a small wharf on the river in a
sea-going launch and that the powerful torch I had
with me was needed to signal a pre-arranged code
for the goods to be brought ashore. She had thereupon jumped to the ridiculous conclusion that the
product was contraband and that I was breaking
the law in some way. The full explanation that I
had to provide as to why this procedure was necessary occupied many weary hours over the weeks
that followed and taxed my powers of invention

to their limit. The trouble was, I suppose, that 'er was over-sensitive to anything that seemed even slightly irregular. In any case, her attitude made storing goods at home, which I'd been reduced to doing for the past year or more, very trying and had severely curtailed the variety of merchandise in which I could safely deal.

So I needed a lock-up not too far from home to make the journey wearisome and not too near to invite the family to use it as a regular port of call. In addition, it naturally had to be large enough to house my impressive stocklist and secure enough to discourage criminals from attempting to remove items without the formality of paying for them. The place needed to be attractive and even inviting since naturally I often needed to use it as a showroom. Items I might need to display varied from Tennessee racoon coats, made from striped polystyrene, to Japanese recreational videos shot in Soho by actors made up so cleverly you'd never guess they wasn't from Yokohama or Osaka but, in the main, Limehouse and Poplar. It must be damp-proof so that no damage would be caused to items like the Daley Daily Diet which was a slimming aid I had perfected which consisted of delicious-looking food that you could eat to your heart's content because it was made exclusively of plastic foam. A week on the Daley Daily Diet and your ribs began to stick out, not to mention your tongue, although reports of hospital admission for a rare kind of poisoning were never vali-dated. All this largesse – and much, much more – needed to be kept in attractive, burglar-proof, con-venient, air-conditioned and humidity-controlled conditions where it could be displayed to dis-criminating buyers by day or, as was preferable with some of the more sensitive items, by night. And until now I had never found such a place in

£ The second rule of life for all those whose business activities sometimes bring them into unfriendly contact with the police is: Don't make waves. (The first is, of course: Don't get caught)

Fulham. Could this be it?

I sat for a long time at the wheel of the Jag gazing in awe at the building that stretched its low, sleek length with a big 'FOR SALE' notice planted in front of it. The more I looked the more convinced I became – correctly I later discovered – that this structure actually did possess all the qualities I have listed above. Could I therefore, as a responsible husband, father and trader, flit away to Australia now that I had at long last discovered the key to fortune, social success and a decent private education for the nippers? There was, of course, one little snag. I had no money with which to purchase this bungaloid dream. I had, in fact, just then somewhat less liquidity than a duck pond in the Sahara. But when had such a trifling obstacle ever hindered a Daley? Two reasonable businessmen can almost always reach an accommodation if the terms are right. So that meant all I needed to do was figure out what terms would be right for inducing the owner of this potential Aladdin's Cave to hand over possession of it to me. I reached forward and thoughtfully turned the ignition switch and starter of the Jaguar and then, already grappling with the problem in the powerful computer that is my brain, made a slow U-turn and then cruised evenly to the Winchester Club for a refreshing vodka and slimline.

Two of these delightful beverages later, I found that the correct starting point for my new venture had become clear to me. This was to go back to what I hoped would soon be my new lock-up and scout around to see if I could spot anything that might further my ambition to acquire the place. It had also occurred to me that I had not yet inspected, even through a window, the interior and clearly I had to make certain that inside too the place was what I wanted.

So back into the driving seat of my sumptuous Jaguar I eased myself and, reversing the direction of travel, glided back to the desired building. I noted approvingly, as I drew near, that the structure was surrounded by a little network of approach roads that would make it hard to seal off if, for some misguided reason, the Old Bill decided that they wished to seal it off. I parked the car in a broad forecourt, which, I again noted approvingly, was very suitable for offloading anything from Bechstein pianos (actually constructed by a genius in Norfolk on an island in the marshes) to boxes of party poppers (both of which, you may be surprised to learn, are fast-selling lines). I walked over to the nearest window and had a butchers. A large interior with smooth concrete floor and no obstacles to partitioning any way I chose, well lit and very clean and fresh-looking, met my minces. I mentally rubbed my hands together in delight. It was perfect. Well now to look – hang about! I peered and then reached up and wiped away a little of the surface dust from the window. Then I peered again. Yes, now I could see the legs of a desk in a little room opening off the main hall. And I could also see that the light in the chamber was on. Apparently someone was on the premises and that someone could easily be the owner. Adrenalin pumped into my system and, straightening up, I went in search of my prey.

At last – the dream lock-up!

I explored the outside of the building and came before long to barred double doors. Without much hope that anything useful would result I pressed the release bars. And to my delight and surprise the doors swung majestically open before me. Feeling somewhat like a monarch about to be crowned, I advanced into the enclosed space and crossed it to the open door I had spotted from without. As I got near I saw that I had been right. It was an office containing a desk. The light was on and from my new vantage point I now saw that on the desk rested a human arm and hand, all of the person within that was visible from my angle of approach.

I advanced softly, anxious to catch a glimpse of the bloke it was my mission to bend to my will. Unguarded first impressions can be very important in business. This chap might, for example, be engaged in some clandestine activity which could have provided me with a little leverage if I had caught him at it. But when I reached the door and peered stealthily round it I saw that the fellow there was simply covering sheet after sheet of paper with calculations. He was youthful, dressed casually, had a broad, slab-like face and piercing blue eyes. Nice pair of shoulders and, best of all, he didn't look too bright. I tapped lightly on the door and his head immediately flipped up and directed a level stare in my direction.

'Saw your "For Sale" notice outside,' I said with my most winning smile. 'May I come in?'

He nodded.

'Yeah, come in.'

As I accepted this roughly-expressed invitation, some little switch clicked on in my mind and my brow wrinkled slightly.

'Don't I know you from somewhere?' I asked, and it was a genuine query, not one aimed at creating a falsely matey effect.

'Dunno. Do you?' he asked indifferently.

I shrugged.

'Oh well, I meet a lot of people. Arthur Daley. You've probably heard of me.'

I reached out a fraternal hand which he took firmly and shook, remarking:

'No.'

'No, what?'

'No. I've never heard of you.'

'New around here, are you?'

'No.'

'Oh well, the point is, I saw your "For Sale" sign outside and I just might be, if the price was right and took full account of the present depressed state of the property market, and if the amenities and facilities was up to the standards I expect and enjoy in my present warehouse, and if you was prepared to make the right terms and discounts – I just might be interested in purchasing it.'

He leaned back in his seat and the ghost of a smile played across his broad, honest features.

'Oh, might you?'

'Yes, I might.'

'Twenty grand.'

'What?'

'Twenty grand. That's the price.'

'Well, it's a much higher bargaining platform than I'd anticipated but –'

'No bargaining. No negotiating. Twenty grand cash or some fully guaranteed paper. That's what I was told to say.'

'Told to say? Am I to understand that you're not the owner of this warehouse?'

He chuckled slightly. There was an air of rude confidence about him which I hadn't perhaps fully noted before.

'Me? I'm just the caretaker.'

I frowned.

'Well, you might have told me. I never talk turkey with the monkey. So where's the organ-grinder?'

His eyes narrowed slightly as if he was about to take offence at my manner. But then he shrugged and smiled.

'Owner's not here. Never comes here. Got an office off the King's Road.'

'I see. Well, if you'll just note down the address for me, I'll pay him a little business call.'

He took a clean scrap of paper and started writing. I tried to make sense of the calculations scattered about on his desk.

'If you're not in business,' I asked. 'What's with the figures?'

'Racing. Give us this day our daily bet.'

'You're very thorough. Does it help?'

'Oh, tremendously. I win very nearly as much as I lose.'

£ I never talk turkey with the monkey

'I try to do a little better than that. Which is why I'm asking what in your opinion would be the best way to approach your employer?'

He shrugged.

'All I know is I've been told to say: no bargains, no quibbles – just twenty grand on the nail.'

'Which you and I both know is totally unrealistic. So if you can suggest some way of cutting that by at least a third there'd be a few sovs in it for you once the contracts was exchanged.'

He shrugged again.

'Like I said – I'm just the hired help.'

'Point taken. So what kind of bloke is the owner? I mean is he solvent or in shtook? Is he liable to crack under pressure? And if so what pressure?'

'You could try holding a gun to his head.'

'I keep that for a last resort. Listen, are you sure I don't know you?'

'No. I'm just sure I don't know you. I've thought of a way you could get this place for a song.'

'I'm all ears.'

'Trouble is you'd have to be Frank Sinatra to sing it. See, the owner's a Greek and he's potty about Frank Sinatra.'

I started.

'Name of Armentides or Aramintides or something like that?' I asked. 'I sold a geezer with a name like that some ex-service field kitchen gear which he used to set up in the restaurant business. Now he's got three kebab joints in Fulham and a couple more in Chelsea.'

'Sure it wasn't Aramintes?'

'That's the one.'

'Then this could be your lucky day. He's the owner.'

We looked at each other with understanding. I unshipped my wallet and, with a casual air, dropped five fifties on the desk in front of him. It was practically my whole worldly wealth but it would have wrecked the air of effortless affluence I'd decided would be the most suitable if he'd so much as suspected it. He didn't reach for the wad but just clocked it with his head slightly on one side.

'So it's not Christmas. Why?'

'Few sovs I promised you too for a good tip. Look, you've got the right physique for it. See at a glance. I don't suppose you're handy with your fists, are you?'

'Why?'

'Just that I've been looking for a new minder for some time. Interested?'

'Not really. I happen to like the shape of my nose.'

'Right, right, frightened of the flying leather. You young fellows are all the same these days. Cowed by the colour scarlet.'

'And what are you then, kinky for punishment?'

I smiled sadly.

'I'm past it now, but I could look after myself when I was a young man. Quite at home with the basic repertoire of punches. So what's the name then?'

'Try Pete. If I wag my tail you've got it right.'

'Very well then, Pete, I'll be seeing you. Oh, it's possible once I've acquired this place I'll need a spot of warehousing and suchlike. Would you be interested in that?'

'You could always give me a bell and try me. This is the number.'

I waited while he scrawled it on a scrap of paper. Then I slipped it into my wallet.

'Right, I'll just pop round and conclude the deal with my old friend Ari – Hari –'

'Aramintes.'

'Exactly. See you, Pete.'

About six months later, I was seated where Pete had been sitting on the occasion I have just been describing, at the desk which was now my desk. There was a kind of wonderland of commerce beyond the office. Racks of shelves and storage bays, holding a wondrous variety of precious things, filled its entire interior. Somewhere in my lock-up you could have found silks from the far East of Manchester, electronic goods and consumer durables made by the world's top manufacturers according to the labels, cases of fine champagne and cognac almost indistinguishable, even by the most discerning palates, from the French kind, bone china more delicate and artistic than Worcester, ladies' coats, hats and undies in the latest fashions, made up in craft workshops in London's East End from designs in *Vogue* magazine, tinned seal-blubber (an experimental line this), a stunning range of plastic furniture for underweight families, electronic dog collars – I could go on all day.

Pete was wheeling in a hand truck holding boxes full of little model animals for nurseries that glowed in the dark – the animals, that is, and not the nurseries. I picked up the dog and dialled for about the tenth time that day. And soon from the instrument

issued the same illiterate electronic voice that I had
been getting every time I dialled: 'Bertrand Baggins
is very sorry to 'ave to inform you that 'e is not at
'ome. This is because 'e 'as 'ad to go out. If you
leave your beep after you 'as 'eard the name – no,
that's not right. I meant, if you leave your name
after you 'as 'eard the beep – or perhaps it should
be bleep – whichever – any old how, Mr Baggins
will give you a beep or a bleep back later when 'e
is once more at 'ome.'

It was about three hours since Dave had called
from the Winchester to say he'd overheard the two
Manzoni Maulers talking about paying me a visit
some time that afternoon. And Baggins was my
current minder. No, I decided at that moment, he
was my ex-minder. Baggins was six foot two and
had biceps like bowling pins but I had never seen
him take on anyone but an inebriated teenager
who was being a little troublesome in a pub and
then it had turned out to be pretty much an even
fight. But the chief factor in my decision to dispense
with Baggins's services was that this was the third
time that he'd let me down when a shoot-out was
approaching. It was as if Doc Holiday, on his way
across Tombstone to join the other glory boys at the
OK Corral, had decided instead to nip down a side-
street and scarper across the Pampas or the prairie
or whatever. Baggins, I decided, was nothing but
a bull artist. He might even be simply a coward
and it will tell you something about the problem of
finding a decent minder when I inform you that, for
all his ghastly faults, Baggins was still the second-
best minder I'd ever had. The best of all, what's
more, had only beaten him by a whisker when
they'd had a fight outside the Rose and Crown
one evening. At that moment I felt like shouting:
'A minder, a minder, my kingdom for a half-way
decent minder.' Only who was there to hear? Only

*Dave slyly
eavesdropping
on the dread
Manzoni Maulers*

the chicken-hearted handyman next door.

I glanced out into the main area of the lock-up where 'chicken-heart' was neatly laying out the little glowing animals for display. Should I appeal to him to rally round his new employer and face the Manzonis? I sighed. Better to rely on my own guile and wit. For I simply could not bring myself to act as prudence kept loudly dictating and scarper. Although the thought of what the Manzonis might do to my person made my blood run cold, the thought of what they might do to my merchandise made it freeze solid.

But who, you are probably wondering, were these fierce Manzonis? They was the emissaries of a powerful local business interest. The Greek Aramintes? Never. The deal for the purchase of my lock-up from Aramintes had gone through with smoothness and ease. Ari, as he had invited me to call him, had been delighted by the opportunity to do me a reciprocal favour. In his spacious and pungent office (situated above the biggest and most up-market of his kebab houses in Chelsea), he had chuckled, slapped me on the back, poured ouzo down my throat, scoured my lungs with a really evil little Greek cigar and finally insisted that I take the lease of the lock-up almost as a gift, agreeing only to pay, on an interest-free basis, whatever I could manage as I found it convenient. Naturally, being a businessman, he had stipulated that if he ever discovered that any other creditor was getting paid before him he would blow up my house and sell my wife and kids into slavery but other than that he promised to put no pressure on me at all. So Ari and I were on cheek-kissing terms.

Then who, you ask once more, was the governor of the dread Manzoni Brothers? The fact is it was their mum, Sophia Manzoni, as wicked a godmother as ever ran half a dozen of the most lucrative rackets in a London borough. Not only did scrap metal merchants have to hand over any gold they found to Sophia Manzoni or run the risk of soon finding a few live hand-grenades amongst the scrap metal but restaurateurs had to pay her what she called a cockroach tax.

'I insist on clear pure food,' she would hiss in the hapless hash-slinger's ear, her two titanic sons flanking her, 'and so from now on you must pay me one hundred pounds for every cockroach found on your premises.' At this point Luigi, the bigger by nearly an inch over his six-foot-five brother, would take a box from his pocket and release from it a small herd of cockroaches while the despairing scampi griller scribbled out a cheque for a huge sum. That was the thing about Sophia. She was ingenious. Not for her merely boring and conventional rackets like protection and prostitution but always novelties such as slippage. For a small weekly sum (to a billionnaire) she would guarantee to minimise the risk that someone would slip and break a bone and thus be in a position to start an action for damages on the premises of a shopkeeper or restaurateur. Those who failed to pay 'slippage' would soon afterwards find a layer of an incredibly slippery substance lining their floors, furniture, counters and ultimately bodies. Any customer bustling hopefully in to make a purchase was almost instantly transformed into a kind of windmill of flying arms and legs. That, at least, was the theory Sophia worked on, but word quite soon got round the trading community that a certain brand of detergent called Foamation neutralised whatever Sophia was using and she quietly dropped 'slippage' from her repertoire. Needless to say, all Sophia's rackets depended crucially on the enforcing powers of her two huge sons for their effectiveness.

So which of her pranks had I run foul of? Oddly enough, none of them. I had simply refused her business overtures. Naturally, she spread the rumour that the affair was romantic and that in her native Sicily I would have been deprived at weekly intervals of some small but significant part of my body until I had fulfilled my original proposal. It was no use my insisting to her that I was a happily married man. She had got it firmly into her head that the night I offered her a lift home from the Rotary Club's annual Binge and Ball at the town hall I had shown romantic interest in her.

I will concede at once that Sophia, while one of the toughest female gangsters in the West, was not a bad looker if you happened to like raven-black hair, lustrous black eyes and big melons. But she was not young and I doubt if the forty-four she admitted to was within hailing distance of the truth. More importantly, my real reason for accompanying Sophia into her superb floating home – a destroyer converted into a palatial suite of rooms moored in the Thames Docks – had been to explore the possibility of a business agreement. But she had only had to open a few of her files for me to realise that it would be like forming a business association with Attila the Hun during one of his expansionist periods. So I backed off smartly.

But after that evening I was continually pestered by Sophia's attentions. It was flattering perhaps, but also a little alarming, when one of the Manzoni brothers arrived by taxi to bring me a bunch of flowers. It became increasingly difficult to convince 'er indoors that they was merely samples for my inspection got up by a florist's shop in which I had an interest. Finally, when Luigi, I think it was, varied the procedure by bringing me a wreath one day, I decided that the time had come to pay a visit to Sophia and get the matter cleared up. But it didn't work. She told me in effect that those who wouldn't wed or woo her must pay her and she put me down for a third of all my profits.

Naturally I had assumed this was a joke – until I received Dave's phone call. I picked up the dog to try Baggins' number just once more – and heard a car grinding to a halt out-side. Dropping the

As wicked a godmother as ever terrorised Fulham

phone like a hot potato I rushed out of my office to the place where Pete was tastefully completing his 'moonlight zoo' which was intended to charm a buyer from a big toyshop who would be paying us a call later in the afternoon.

'They're here!' I announced in a voice that struck me as somewhat more high-pitched than the one normally used.

'Who's here?' asked Pete, shifting a tiny hippo-potamus about a quarter of an inch with an artistic forefinger.

'The Manzonis.'

He glanced round at this. The name was clearly one with which he was familiar.

'What, the Sicilian slaughterers? What do they want?'

'A few pints of my blood.'

He touched a giraffe but changed his mind and didn't actually move it.

'Why? What you done to them?'

'I ain't done nothing to them. It's their mon-strous mum, Sophia. You know what she's like.'

'Charming Italian lady, the buzz goes. Never met her myself.'

'She's charming like Lucretia Borgia. She has the social graces of Lady Macbeth. And her boys is both in the Kray class with a dash of Frankenstein's monster thrown in. This is the time, Pete.'

He glanced at his watch.

'Nearly five. I'll be knocking off soon. Now about the wages you owe –'

'Pete, my blood is about to darken the floor you're standing on and you're thinking of filthy lucre? Talking of which, there's a hundred sovs in it for you if you stand by me.'

He shook his head.

'Warehouseman,' he said firmly.

'But, couldn't you just – Oh my gawd, here they is!'

At the clang of the big double doors, which I suddenly remembered I had neglected to lock, I turned in panic. Pete too glanced up from the three little pigs he was arranging. And it was indeed an interesting, if terrible, sight which met our eyes. Darkening the aisle down which they lurched came two gigantic figures, whose joint shoulder width was practically that of a tank and whose evil scowls cast a pall over the daylight itself.

'Pete, two hundred sovs! Help me!'

I have often congratulated myself since that moment that I did not actually sink to my knees and hug his legs. I would not be ashamed to admit it if I had done so for, although I am no coward and have acquitted myself well in numerous threatening situations, the advancing duo would have struck terror into the heart of a David. And I hadn't even got a slingshot with which to try and bean one of them, although the other would doubtless then have instantly reduced me to catsmeat.

'Pete, three hundred!'

'No way,' he said firmly.

And at that moment, Luigi, I think it was, or

possibly Giuseppe, gave voice with a sound like the Hound of the Baskervilles coming over the top of Blood Tor.

The M-M-M-Manzonis!

'Five thousand quid,' he bayed. 'You owe our mama.'

'Pay!' howled the other. 'Or we beat you up.'

Even as a thrill of sheer terror sped like liquid ice through my veins, I felt a slight sense of let-down at the giant's feeble language. 'Beat you up'? That was pretty unimpressive for two such spectacular monsters. Still the process itself would doubtless make up for any weakness in its description.

Then came my moment, the memory of which has ever since sustained me when I have had occasion to doubt my own courage. Although it took a tremendous effort of will to force what was not much better than a squeak to my lips, I managed it.

'Not on, Giuseppe,' I squeaked. 'And I apolo-

gise if you're really Luigi. I don't owe your charming mother a single sov. And there's nothing you
can do about it.'

'Yes, there is,' affirmed Luigi gently. 'I can
break every bone you got.'

He thereupon reached down a Parma ham –
well, it was probably a human hand but it looked
much like the famous Italian delicacy – uncoiled
five immense salamis from it, which might have
been fingers, closed them on my collar and lifted
me several feet in the air.

'Oi,' said an irritated voice from behind him.
'Careful of my zoo.'

Intrigued, Luigi replaced me on the tarmac
and turned to see who'd suddenly come over
suicidal. He beheld Pete giving him a frown of
displeasure.

'What?' asked Luigi.

'You knocked over this gazelle,' Pete specified,
pointing at the dainty glass beast which was lying
pathetically on its side.

'Really?' said Luigi. 'Maybe it like company –'

He reached out a Parma ham and swept off
the shelf all the other animals that Pete had so
laboriously positioned. They went flying across the
lock-up, many of them shattering as they came
down and hit the hard floor.

'That was very stupid and destructive,' said Pete
with a deep sigh as if at the inexhaustible depths of
human folly.

'Shut up,' suggested Luigi.

He thereupon turned back to me and once
more performed the crane operation which carried
me several feet into the sky. Then he carefully drew
back his Parma – his fist – clearly with the intention
of propelling me over a bank of shelves and then
down onto the concrete floor beyond it. But at just
this moment Pete tapped him gently on the shoul-

der. Even as I murmured a few prayers that I had learned at my mother's knee, I marvelled at Pete's temerity. If I'd been him, I'd have given the whole sordid squabble a miss and gone home for the night without even sweeping up the broken glass animals. Luigi seemed intrigued by Pete's perseverance and even went so far, as he replaced me on the hard floor, of uttering what for him must have been a hilariously witty remark.

'What?' he asked. 'You want a flying lesson too?'

Without waiting for an answer, he hurled his huge fist straight at Pete's mace. However, Pete's defensive instinct proved to be in excellent working order. At the instant when Luigi's Parma ham burned through the space where Pete's head had been but a moment before the item was no longer there but about a yard to the right.

'What?' grunted Luigi, clearly outraged by this mishap. And a moment later his outrage must have been considerably increased when a smaller fist than his own, but one travelling with about the velocity of an artillery shell, connected squarely with his jaw. Luigi was large and it is only true, as the old saying has it, that the larger they are the harder they fall, if they really do fall. Luigi didn't. But he did stagger backwards quite a long way. And when he came to a halt the expression on his face, as he gazed at his unexpected antagonist, showed dawning respect. Pete, however, had no time to take a bow, for now Giuseppe, clearly irritated by the damage that had been inflicted on his brother, joined the fray.

Well, it lasted for about six minutes in all. Mercifully the Manzonis between them managed to land only one good punch but that one, the work of Giuseppe, was enough to shift Pete a good three feet into the air and then over a counter to land in a cascade of toppling steel money boxes. The dazed lad then lay where he had fallen for a few seconds, clearly out of touch with events, only to recover just as Giuseppe, whose forwards lumber was fearsome but far from rapid, hauled him to his feet again. At this, to my astonished delight, Pete unleashed a left upper cut which did not actually raise the giant from the floor but caused his gingerbread to rock backwards and forwards like a metronome. And after that it was really just a tidying up operation by Pete which made the Manzonis very untidy indeed.

'Okay,' grunted Giuseppe, having concluded that victory was somehow eluding them.

'All right,' gasped Luigi, suspecting that he and his brother must, at best, be down on points.

'Enough,' they both implored.

'Quite enough,' I added firmly. 'I hereby declare that this contest is over and what's more so is the war. Give your delightful mother the happy news, will you, boys? And tell her that in future we might do business together if she ever decides to dabble in anything legal.'

'All right,' agreed Giuseppe, making certain his front teeth were all still firmly installed in his jaw.

'Okay,' conceded Luigi, fingering his ear as if under the impression that it might be expanding.

And a few minutes later Pete and I watched their car swing around in a U-turn and then trundle away down the drive.

I said:

'It's not Pete, is it? It's Terry McCann.'

'What makes you think so?'

'Funny thing, I thought I knew your jem mace when I first come in here. But it was the uppercut I recognised when you was applying it to Giuseppe just now. Saw you fight two or three times in the old days. So why the incognito?'

'Because I am not in the muscle business any more. Soon as you started going on about needing a minder I knew I needed a cover or you'd have been at me day and night.'

'So what made you bring the muscle into play just now?'

'Can't stand having my work ruined, can I?'

I smiled knowingly.

'More important, you're good and you need a work-out now and then. I'll see you get it from now on.'

''Ang about. I meant what I said –'

'Course you did. But what you said and what you just did is two very different things. You can go on fiddling with glass animals to your heart's content. I don't need muscle very often but when I do it's nice to know that from now on I'll have the best.'

'I'm not promising –'

'No need. We'll shake on it. We're both gentlemen. And we'll have a drink to seal the compact.'

I took from a shelf above my head two glasses and a bottle labelled 'Yokohama Velly Old Malt

His gingerbread rocked like a metronome

Scotch Wiskee' and poured us a noggin each. I explained:

'Naturally I relabel this stuff for the English market. Cheers, Terry.'

He shook his head doubtfully but I could see that his blue eyes was amused. Considering the state of the Goliaths he'd recently toppled he looked amazingly unscarred. We clinked glasses and as I brought mine to my lips I thought: Now I've got the best lock-up and also the best minder in the whole of Fulham. So from here on it's got to be straight up and don't stop till you touch heaven.

'Come on, Terry. Plenty more.'

He took a sip. I didn't in the least mind the look of strangled distress that appeared on his face. The Yokohama often affected people like that first time. He'd get used to it.

A drink for the best minder in Fulham

CHAPTER FIVE
THE HELPING HAND

'**H**OW DO YOU DO IT, ARTHUR?' I am often asked. 'Why is it that whenever I am out and about with you in Fulham people is continually coming up and thanking you for some kind or thoughtful act that you have performed? How does it happen that the poor and the needy often clasp your hand reverently and press it gratefully? Why do I so often hear your name spoken in hushed and appreciative tones?'

It is no use me protesting that charitable deeds have always been undertaken by enlightened businessmen, and that, when I extend my helping hand, I am merely acting in a well-trodden tradition. No, the questioner will not buy this. He continues:

'Take Sid, the fixer – no one thrusts flowers through his car windows or stands on the kerb and claps as his grotty old Ford goes banging past like they do when you glides down the street in your Jaguar saloon. Do not pretend, Arthur, that you are just like other successful merchants in this parish when the truth is that your benevolence is often the last hope of the downtrodden.

I then reply:

'This is hard to believe. Are you sure of your facts?'

'It is common knowledge, Arthur. So what is your secret?'

And what indeed can it be? I have puzzled over this question many times and the only answer I can come up with is: a feeling heart. Unlike most people I have always been blessed, or, as some selfish

£ There was something about the thin, ferrety one that suggested to me that this time a really high-grade bloodhound was on the trail of Arthur Daley

hustlers would think, cursed with a feeling heart which propels me in the direction of helping my fellow men and I include in that group, since I am certainly no chauvinist, my fellow women too.

But what saddens me is how rarely opportunities to do good arise. I go on trying to plug gaps in the social services wherever I can and there is no doubt that seeing a coachload of pensioners setting off with eager smiling faces for Clacton or Southend on a day's coach-trip which I am subsidising causes me huge satisfaction. Likewise I feel a warm glow of self-congratulation when I attend street parties for the kiddies which I have financed. I make sure only wholesome organic cakes and jellies are served and I also hire the very best conjurors and clowns that ever put a 'having a Big Success on the End of Blackpool Pier' advertisement in *The Stage* to entertain the little perishers.

But such generous deeds, I am well aware, hardly get to the heart of the problem. There is a whole heap of human suffering out there which makes me choke back a tear whenever I think about it. And it is because I have long been tormented by the paucity of my feeble efforts in the face of this challenge that I was so gratified by an encounter I had with a crusty old bugger in a boozer a year or two ago. I have to say at the outset that if I had known of the maelstrom of intrigue and even persecution in which I became involved as a result of this meeting I might have thought twice about taking up his cause. But at the time I was merely blinded by a vision of doing good. It happened like this:

I was lunching in the Cricketer off a ploughman's and a voddy when I accidentally knocked a half pint of bitter off the counter with my elbow. This produced a strangled curse and I turned to

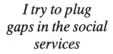

I try to plug gaps in the social services

see a malevolent old jem mace glaring at me.

'Oops!' I exclaimed with a sympathetic shrug. 'Lucky it was only a half.'

'All I can afford is a half,' growled the rough old fellow, scowling.

'Oh dear, down on our luck, are we?'

'Yes, we are. As we will continue to be for the rest of our miserable lives. Because we are opes. Do you know what an ope is?'

'From Central Asia, is it? Just south of the Caucasus?'

'From Fulham, just south of Kensington. An ope is an old age pensioner, sonny. And we are expected to feed, clothe ourselves and refresh our lifelong thirst on a pittance that would not keep a koala bear in eucalyptus leaves. Well, are you going to buy me the half you knocked off the counter or aren't you?'

Naturally, my deep sense of justice raised its

head at this.

'Hang about,' I urged the surly ancient, 'if you hadn't put it practically up against my coat sleeve I wouldn't have knocked it over. I don't reckon it's down to me.'

'No, you wouldn't,' he sneered. 'That's why you've got that nice camelhair coat on. The rich hang on to what they've sweated out of the likes of us. Well, I can't afford another half. So I'll get back to my sixty-watt bulb and single-bar electric fire. But it's not the material things that rankle most. It's being useless. It's being denied the chance to practise my trade.'

'And just what would that trade be?' I called after him as he shuffled away.

He turned back.

'Plasterer. Best in South London, I was. Won the Plasterer's Cup, which was first awarded in the reign of Henry the Sixth, two years running. And now, although my hand has lost none of its cunning, I couldn't get a job lining a ruddy outhouse because I'm considered too bloody OLD! I hope your drink chokes you.'

'Yes, and your very good health too – hang about!'

A dazzling idea had suddenly exploded in my mind. A plasterer? When was it? Last week some time – yes, got it! I'd been delivering a big-screen television to a house in Weps Lane and something had crunched under my feet.

'Plaster fell off the ceiling,' said the plump lady of the house tartly. 'It was only done two months ago. Can't get nothing done properly these days.'

As I staggered with my burden into her drawing room I sympathised.

'That's 'cause they're not properly trained. No proper apprentice system any more. No real exams or certificates. Your modern skilled workman is basically just a yob with a bag of multi-purpose tools. If plumbers is in short supply they is all suddenly experts at pipe-work. If what's in demand is chippies, suddenly everyone can make a lovely dove-tail joint. Give me the old days when an English tradesman was the best in the world and sweated honest toil for every sov he earned. That'll be five hundred pounds please, and in cash as we agreed.'

'Could you connect it up for me?'

'Wish I could spare the time, my love, but I've got three more to deliver before lunch. But there's no problem. You just push that gidget there into this plug here and attach all these wires in the different holes according to what colour they are and you could be in time to watch the boat race. No, no cheques I'm afraid. Strictly cash.'

A plasterer! In addition to an electrician that good housewife had urgently required a plasterer and she hadn't been able to find one. I called out to the crusty old bugger who was once more on his way to the door.

'Don't rush off. What was you drinking? Bitter? Have a pint on me – well, say a half to kick off with. So you is eating your heart out to get back into harness and start slapping the pink goo about, are you?'

The upshot was that I phoned the lady I'd delivered the television to and was a bit distressed to find that she'd had a small fire on the premises. At first she was inclined to be hostile towards me but I finally convinced her that she couldn't have followed the colour coding of the wires correctly. From that point it was but a small step to ascertaining that she still needed a plasterer. Indeed she needed one more than ever because the wall behind the television set was now cracked and scorched. I gave her the good news.

'I think I have just the man – no, don't hang
up. This is a real craftsman, someone who twice
won the Plasterer's Cup which, as you probably
know, is the same one that was originally given
by Henry the Eighth to the bloke that did the
royal bedchamber which, as you can imagine,
got a lot of wear and tear. I'll get him to call
round in the morning. And don't worry about
terms. They will be purely nominal. All I am
interested in is bringing you two together. He is
yearning to practise his craft and you is yearning
to have it practised. Just one thing: these crafts-
men is very haughty about money matters, so
don't mention anything about fees to him. I am
his appointed agent and you will receive my bill
in due course.'

*Nothing to fear
from the Old Bill*

I think it is safe to say that of all the phil-
anthropic activities I have engaged upon in my
whole professional life none has given me such
deep and enduring satisfaction as what I consider
my veterans' reclamation scheme. Of course, it is
very far from the case that every retired working
man wants nothing better than to hoist his tool
bag again and set off for a hard day's labour. But
it is equally true that a sizeable proportion wants
nothing better. They never learn the arts of leisure.
Not for them golf or even bar billiards. They have
no taste for hobbies or reading or listening to good
music. Their whole being yearns to get back under
the floorboards and unblock the sink trap or draw
wires through holes in the walls or plonk bricks on
top of each other. All their days is consumed in
nostalgia for the wonderful old times when their
whirling electric saws cut and shaped planks and
the air rang to the sounds of their lusty hammers.
For such men, retirement is worse than death.
It is living decay. And it was this that I saved
them from.

You should see my stacks of thank-you letters. They fill twenty-seven shoe boxes. I guarantee that no one but a hard-hearted brute could read a few at random without feeling a suspicious moisture in the corner of his eye at this testimony to human gratitude. 'Dear Arthur' is the least complimentary way they begin. More often it is 'Dear Friend', quite often even 'Dear Benefactor' and one veteran wallpaper hanger, almost crazed with joy, actually addressed his missive to me (containing a fifty-pound note which, of course, I immediately returned to him) 'Dear Saviour' which was perhaps a bit over the top although his wife, writing separately, testified that the poor old sod had been lapsing into premature senility and alcoholism before I charitably found him a hotel to paper.

For three years the torrent of grateful post continued to provide a daily current of warmth in my life. Each morning 'er and I would open the envelopes with trembling fingers knowing that we was about to be profoundly moved by the heartfelt gratitude of simple, honest fellows. For three years the 'ope' population of Fulham enjoyed a level of happiness which was the envy of the nation. And then, almost unbelievably, the short-sighted authorities put a stop to it!

Why, I hear you cry out in dismay, oh why did this wonderful scheme of social rehabilitation not grow and spread? Why was it brutally abandoned? And the answer – which with heavy heart I will now relate – testifies to the greed, suspicion and envy of petty men what has the power to persecute us visionaries. The first intimation I had that all was not right with my veterans came when Terry strode into the lock-up one day with the terse query:

''Ere, what you been up to now?'

I looked up at him with a puzzled smile from the papers I had been working on.

'I'm sorry?' I asked patiently. 'What was that query, Terence?'

'What's the Old Bill want with you?'

Without ceasing to smile I raised an eyebrow slightly.

'The constabulary? I cannot imagine. Why do you ask?'

'One come round this morning when you was out. Plain-clothes. Asked if this was the HQ of the Veterans' Brigade. What the hell's the Veterans' Brigade?'

'An organisation I run to help ease the trauma of retirement for honest workmen.'

His eyes narrowed.

'What you mean a tax fiddle, like your coach outings and street parties?'

I sighed.

'You must learn to grasp the distinction, Terry, between tax avoidance and tax evasion. The former, perfectly legal, activity I practise with as much skill and enthusiasm as any businessman in Fulham and this helps me to finance my large range of charitable activities.'

'Yeah, yeah and these veterans – are they bent or what?'

'The Veterans' Brigade is a lifeline for many of the prematurely superannuated tradesmen of Fulham.'

'But what's in it for you?'

'The satisfaction of seeing fulfilled men and smiling women. The joy of reclaiming prime human material.'

'I meant: how much loot?'

'The organisation is non-profit-making. As my books will confirm.'

I opened a drawer in my desk and lifted out several heavy ledgers.

'And if,' I resumed placidly, 'the officer of the

law should return, you are at liberty to tell him, yes, this is the headquarters of the Veterans' and to allow him to peruse and inspect these records to his heart's content.'

Terry turned through the ledger with disbelief written all over his face.

'Tenner, tenner, tenner – is that it then? They all get a tenner?'

'That's right, a tenner a day to provide them with a far better lifestyle than their idle neighbours who do not participate in the scheme. But best of all, it permits them to continue practising their craft and thus to maintain their pride. I can tell you this, Terence, there has never been a more imaginative or effective scheme for restoring –'

''Ang about. 'Ere 'e is again,' said Terry with a frown, looking out of the window. 'And 'e's got someone with him.'

I also stood up and looked in the direction he was looking. Walking towards us from an unmarked Ford came two men. One was moon-faced and bespectacled and the other looked very like a ferret. They were unmistakably plain-clothes detectives as could be established from their regulation detectives' suits and raincoats turned out by a special clothing factory located somewhere in New Scotland Yard, and that peculiar strut which seems to proclaim: Pretend you haven't penetrated our disguise or we'll find something to book you with.

Over the preceding years I had suffered a few regrettable encounters with the local CID but nothing that had resulted in really hard feelings on either side. I realised that, for some extraordinary reason, they had marked me down as someone to be watched, but realised this was probably only because my wide range of commercial activities was something they had never encountered before and which thus activated their suspicious natures. The baselessness of their suspicions was proved by the fact that, although I had been hauled in for questioning on several occasions, I had never been charged with anything. I was a citizen without a blemish on my character. And yet – as I watched these two approaching – a faint sense of foreboding rose up inside me. There was something about the thin, ferrety one – something about the way his sharp-featured head swivelled abruptly this way and that, something about the position of his hands jammed into his raincoat pockets, as if to keep them from either pummelling a cringing villain or ripping out his own hair in frustration – something that suggested to me that this time a really high-grade bloodhound was on the trail of Arthur Daley.

'Hello,' said the moon-faced man, entering first. 'I've brought Sergeant Chisholm to meet you.'

The ferret now smiled but succeeded in doing so without any use of his eyes. These orbs he kept occupied in darting suspicious glances all over my impressive lock-up. He was, however, impeccably polite.

'Arthur Daley, I believe?' he said, extending his hand.

I smiled, took it and tried to suppress a shudder at finding that it felt like a loose cluster of ice-cold bones. Chisholm turned to my colleague.

'And Terry McCann, isn't it? I believe you're no stranger to the queen's hospitality, Mr McCann?'

Terry did not deign to answer.

'Anyway,' continued Chisholm, 'I gather you've already met my colleague and carmate, the Welsh wizard of crime investigation, Detective Constable Jones?'

Unmistakably a plain clothes detective

So Terry and I nodded civilly at the moon-faced chap who looked bereft of anything much in the way of faculties.

'And what line of business do you pursue on these impressive premises, Mr Daley?' asked the ferret-like detective.

I beamed as hard as I could.

'As you see, Mr Chisholm, I'm a general trader. This is my merchandise.'

'All above board?' asked the other, beginning to edge away along one of the aisles. 'All properly invoiced and receipted? All relevant taxes paid? All imported goods accompanied by valid import licences and ditto for exports? All fair and square, Mr Daley?'

'Naturally, Mr Chisholm. Goes without saying.'

Chisholm picked up a carton of Bulgarian booze which was one of my new lines. He frowned.

'Hm. Isn't "Cognac" a controlled brand name? Isn't it illegal to sell a spirituous liquor called Cognac if it doesn't originate in a specific region of France?'

'You is clearly a wine connoisseur, Mr Chisholm. And what a treat it is to meet another. And, of course, you is perfectly right. But if you just glance at that case again you will see that it contains Bulgarian "Conyac", with a "y". "Conyac" with a "y" is a totally different bevvy from the Frog firewater. It is distilled in the mountains of Bulgaria from rare herbs and flowers and is highly prized by discriminating tipplers.'

'Oh, very amusing. We'll see what Excise have to say about it. And what have we here? Garden gnomes from Venezuela? Made by Incas perhaps? For discriminating gardeners? You certainly go in for variety, Mr Daley.'

'Finest selection of top-class trade goods in South London, Mr Chisholm.'

'Good. Well, I shall maintain a watching brief on your stock from now on, Mr Daley. It's only fair to tell you that I am here to stay. From now on your patch is my patch. And now perhaps you'd tell me all about this Veterans' scam?'

I frowned.

'Scam? Scam? Correct me if I'm wrong, Mr Chisholm, but isn't that a word that means something of doubtful legality? Say, a confidence trick or something of that kind?'

'Your innocence of these murky depths does you credit, Mr Daley. But you have, in fact, put your finger on it. A scam, in the sense that I'm using the term, does in fact mean a confidence trick.'

I shook my head in obvious bewilderment.

'You've lost me, Mr Chisholm. The Veterans' Brigade is one of my charitable enterprises. It is a non-profit-making scheme for helping retired tradesmen who are still in full possession of their physical and mental faculties to ward off the tedium of retirement by practising their craft and at the same time putting a little extra cash in their pockets to provide them with a few of the comforts of life.'

Chisholm, beaming like a steel trap, raised his hands and clapped heartily.

'Oh, bravo, Mr Daley. Very touching and not a little heart-warming. I take it you have books which will substantiate your claim that this Veterans' Brigade is in fact non-profit-making?'

I pulled open the desk drawer with a smooth, carefree action and withdrew the relevant ledgers. Chisholm cast a suspicious eye on them.

'And are these the original or the expurgated versions, Mr Daley?'

I mixed a few drops of hurt expression into the puzzled glance I now shot him.

Chisholm and Jones profane my sacred lock-up

'You've lost me again, Mr Chisholm. But if you care to examine those records, I think you'll find –'

Chisholm reached down, opened a ledger at random, glanced at the page that met his eyes and then, to my surprise, flipped the book shut again.

'It'll keep, Mr Daley. Let's just regard this visit as a preliminary encounter, enabling us to get the measure of each other, shall we? I'm quite sure there'll be many opportunities for us to deepen our acquaintance in the future.'

With a nod of his head and a smile in which his mouth participated but his eyes retained their resemblance to the tips of gun barrels he turned and strode smartly away. The effect was spoiled a little by his having to turn a moment later and, placing his hands on his hips in unconcealed exasperation, bark at his subordinate who was gazing at my shelves with an expression as near to being totally blank as a human being can manage.

'Will you delight me with your continued company, Jones? Or have you elected to throw in your lot with Mr Daley's garden gnomes?'

'Eh? Oh, sorry –' drawled the Welsh rozzer in his mellow sing-song voice. He turned and lumbered after his chief. Terry and I accompanied the two sleuths to the door and watched them enter their car. And then, with me managing a little smile and wave, we watched them drive away. As soon as they were out of sight, I tottered back to my desk and collapsed into my tilting, executive chair. I stretched out a trembling hand.

'Voddy.'

'What?' asked Terry.

'Vodka. There's a bottle – somewhere. I know – it's in the elephant-foot umbrella stand. So that, Terence, is how a chicken must feel when it sees Colonel Saunders striding across the road towards it.'

'Rattle you, did he?'

'He's the real thing, Terry. He's not a Disneyland cop like the others. He means business.'

'Yeah, but if you've nothing to hide –'

'He'll do it for me. And then he'll find it and book me for having hidden it. That bloodhound's out to get me, Terry. Go down to the town hall and enquire about assisted passages –'

'Oh, turn it in.'

'You don't understand. I've only ever seen eyes like that once before and they was on a king cobra. That sleuth would make a Canadian mounted policeman seem like an aimless drifter. Thanks.'

Terry had placed a glass one third full of Vodka on the desk in front of me. I raised it and took a substantial swig.

'Thank God for the Russians. That's put a bit of spirit back into me. Get it? Put a bit of spirit –'

'Yeah, yeah, yeah –' grunted the other impatiently. 'What was it you wanted me to do this afternoon?'

'Hm? Oh, them boxes that came yesterday. They is to be stacked at the far end by the window. I fear it means you'll have to restack some of the other stuff but there's nowhere else for them to go. So you get on with that and I'll be back in a couple of hours.'

With which I finished the glass and felt several degrees better still. What was his name? Chisholm? Well, it would take more than the likes of Detective Sergeant Chisholm and his Welsh zombie assistant to get the better of Arthur Daley.

'Where you going then?' asked Terry.

'Oh, just to water my scams. If the filth return, try to flog them some of those Chinese fighting sticks we laid in for the juvenile delinquent market. Tell them they're a lot more effective than their obsolete truncheons.'

'Oh, ha ha,' said Terry mirthlessly and went out to stack boxes.

Over the next few weeks, however, I began to think that perhaps I'd exaggerated the threat posed by Detective Sergeant Chisholm. No more visits from him. No harassment. No contact at all except once when, issuing from Sasthi Patel's newsagent and tobacconist's with a fresh supply of panatellas, I heard a voice cutting through the roar of traffic like a knife:

'Morning, Mr Daley. Trust your business empire is prospering?'

I glanced up in time to see an inconspicuous car that had just slid past in the traffic flow. Peering back from a lowered window was a face that wore a smile like the East wind. Naturally, I smiled and waved back but afterwards found myself shivering convulsively for several seconds. Still by the end of three weeks I definitely felt that the danger was receding. And, naturally, just as always happens, it was then that the terrible blow fell.

It started innocently enough with Terry and I heaving a dirty great refrigerator into a terraced house in Lamorna Road. Normally, of course, I did not deign to lug merchandise about in person. On this occasion, however, Curly Samson, who I usually slung a bob or two at to give Terry a hand on these occasions, had come down with an attack of alcohol poisoning and was out of action. Since the lady of the house we was delivering to was a regular customer in desperate need of a fridge-freezer to save her frozen goods which was thawing rapidly I had graciously consented to do the menial bit.

'Morning, Mrs Olive,' I puffed as we staggered through her front door with the boxed machine. 'Where do you want it?'

She was of Greek descent, was Mrs Olive, as was her husband, and in spite of having lived in Fulham since she was a young bride, she spoke somewhat quaint English.

'It go in the kitchen, you know, Mr Daley. You must put it quick before my freezies all get hot.'

'Yes, well, we mustn't have your freezies getting hot. Where's the kitchen?'

'Down here where the passage stop. You find nothing. The fridge, the microwave – they even take the cooker – good electric cooker. They take everything.'

'Who take everything, Mrs Olive?'

'The very bloody thieves, Mr Daley.'

'Oh dear! 'Fraid can't talk any more just now. Not really up to this lark. Come on, Terry.'

So we humped and heaved the big, heavy box down into her small kitchen adjoining her little back garden and placed it where she wanted. When it was in place, I glanced about.

'It's no wonder you had a visit from the light-fingered mob, Mrs Olive. They could just stroll in through that hole in the wall.'

'Damned true, Mr Daley. I have the workman in to put in a wet patch.'

'Eh? Oh, you mean damp course.'

'To stop the wet come up. And so the very bloody thieves come hopping in. Still no matter too much. Insurance pay for everything. About high time we get new things, I think.'

'So you're satisfied, Mrs Olive?'

'Happy like sand lady. And is good for you too, Mr Daley.'

'Oh? How's that?'

'It mean you get another customer.'

Naturally, I pricked up my ears.

'Really? Well, if it's a good one there may be a little drink – that is a nice jar of extra-virgin olive oil in it for you, Mrs Olive. Tell me more.'

'This defective comes in to chase the thieves and he says, "Why is big hole in the wall?" So I tell him about the damp patch and he says must be damned stupid workman to leave big hole for thieves. And I say, "No, very good workman from Mr Daley's Veterans but quite old man. He cannot block up hole every night. But very good workman."'

It was like one of those terrible freezing mists they get in Siberia which stops car engines dead in their tracks and turns polar bears into statues. For a moment I found difficulty in catching my breath and I noticed that Terry too looked as if his state of health was no great improvement on a parrot's.

'What was this detective's name, Mrs Olive?'

'Name? Detectives have name? I don't know name. Thin man, thin face and number two man have round face with bespectacles.'

The temperature dropped another hundred degrees or so.

'Tell me about it, Mrs Olive,' I asked softly.

'Detective smile with sharp smile and say, "This is very good news, lady, because I need good workman for wall in my police station. Difficult find good workman. How much does he cost this workman?"'

'And you told him?'

'Yes, of course. I told him is very cheap with Mr Daley's Veterans. Just thirty pounds each day and –'

'When did this occur, Mrs Olive?'

'Just now – before you bring fridge. Where you go, Mr Daley?'

'Urgent job I just remembered, Mrs Olive. You'll love that fridge. Come along, Terence. It's drive like the wind time!'

As we roared and twisted through the traffic in Terry's old banger, which I always use for deliveries of large items in order to spare my Jag, he just wouldn't let up.

'Thirty sovs a day! You grasping old scrooge! And you give the poor sods who get the backache and bang their fingers with hammers a miserable ten! If that's a charitable institution then Parkhurst's a funfair!'

'Terence, Terence, will you never understand about overheads and profit margins –'

'Two hundred sodding per cent!'

'But you is forgetting the risk factor, which is exactly what we is facing at this moment. Five years incarceration cuts down one's earnings something cruel.'

'Still no cause to panic. Chisholm doesn't know what a pittance you pay your geriatric dwarves.'

'Chisholm's bound to have a photographic memory. He looked in my ledger. He'll have seen what my standard rate is. So he'll be getting a search warrant at this very moment so he can come round

That sleuth would make a Canadian mounted policeman seem like an aimless drifter

and sniff out the other set of books.'

The car rocked as Terry flung round his head to glare at me in fury.

'Other set of books? So you admit the whole thing's a scam?'

'I do not. It's just that when I applied for listing as a registered charity I was unjustly turned down because one of the commissioners had heard some ridiculous and mendacious rumours about me. So I had to do it clandestine, didn't I? I owed it to the pensioners not to chicken out and leave them gasping for work like a landed fish gasps for oxygen. I'm no quitter, Terry.'

'Not while there's still a sov to be netted, no. And Chisholm had it sussed out right from the start. Two sets of books. So where do you hide the cooked ones?'

'You'll see. I only pray that you do see before Chisholm does. Won't this banger do more than twenty?'

About six minutes later I gave a sigh of relief as we turned into the last drive leading to the lock-up and were able to perceive that there was no car stationed outside. When we reached the double doors it was clear that they hadn't been tampered with and when we entered my lovely Aladdin's cave of delights, it was plain that it had not been the victim of a brutal police search. Everything was as it should be, including the happy rows of Venezuelan garden gnomes all grinning cheekily down at us. Having led Terry to this part of the lock-up, I counted along one row of gnomes and then down one of the files and picked up the gnome on that spot. I raised it above my head and smashed it to the floor.

'Why take it out on the gnomes?' asked Terry, eyeing me narrowly. 'It's Chisholm you have to face.'

'You needn't look at me like that, Terence. In spite of daily aggravations that might unhinge a lesser man, I am in full possession of my senses. So perhaps you'd be good enough to stoop and remove from the wreckage of that gnome what we tycoons of the electronic age call a floppy disk. Take it down to the river, tie a brick round its neck and chuck it in. It is the only item of incriminating evidence around here and once it has been disposed of we have nothing to fear from a police search, even by Sergeant Chisholm.'

Terry poked about in the rubble of the gnome with the toe of his foot.

'There's nothing there,' he announced.

'Don't be silly. I placed it in the gnome myself, just last week, in anticipation of just such an emergency.'

Terry frowned slightly.

'Last week? But the gnomes have all been moved round since then.'

Have you ever actually felt yourself going pale? I did when Terry said that. Reaching out for support I knocked a silver-gilt picture frame off a shelf.

'How do you mean "moved round"?' I demanded

We have nothing to fear from Chisholm

hoarsely.

'Them Swiss-type watches you wanted stored discreetly, remember? I had to shift the gnomes to get at the secret compartment.'

I remembered.

'Oh my gawd! All of them? You moved all of them?'

'Well no, not all of them. But I can't remember which ones I moved and which I didn't. Seems I moved the one with your floppy dooda in it.'

'Terry, please, concentrate. The gnome that was on this spot. Try and remember where you put it.'

'How the hell can I? They all look alike. And I can't be sure which ones I shifted and which I didn't.'

'But there must be five hundred. More! Five gross, that's what we ordered. What are you doing?'

He had his hand up a gnome's backside.

'Feeling if there's anything inside.'

'No time for that. We'll just have to smash them all.'

'What?'

'If we don't break these gnomes, Tel, they're sure as hell going to break us.'

It was like a Russian boozing party to end all Russian boozing parties. For the next three quarters of an hour the day was made hideous with the sound of breaking gnomes and the curses of Terry and me when each successive victim failed to disgorge a floppy disk from its plaster entrails. And then we both paused as a single gnome-smasher at the sinister sound we had been dreading, which was that of a car pulling up outside. I began to say:

'Looks like it's all –'

But I was interrupted by a yell from Terry.

'Look!'

'What?'

'The floppy dooda. Over there. It must have fallen wide. That's it, isn't it?'

I looked where he was pointing.

'That's it. Quick, Terry!'

He darted over to where the incriminating item lay and scooped it up. At the same moment there came a pounding on the door of the sort only made by triumphant rozzers convinced they have got some wretch in their snares.

'The back way, Terry!' I snapped. 'And like lightning.'

And I took up a gnome and smashed it to the ground. Terry gaped.

'What the hell you doing? We've got the bad-news floppy –'

'Never you mind. Just get the hell out of here.'

Shaking his head at what he took to be my lunatic actions, Terry sprinted up the aisle and out the door leading to the passage and the back exit. As he did so the main door yielded to bolt cutters applied to its padlock and swung open. Instantly Detective Sergeant Chisholm, backed by a panting Welsh copper, bounded towards me like starving greyhounds. The key question was: had they or had they not seen Terry making his hasty exit? I raised another gnome and, as Chisholm and Jones screeched to a halt, smashed it on the concrete in front of them.

'Hate garden gnomes, do we, Mr Daley?' barked Chisholm, stirring the rubble of the gnome I had just smashed with the toe of his shoe. I breathed a secret sigh of relief. Clearly he couldn't have spotted Terry.

'Social conscience, Mr Chisholm,' I explained, shaking my head mournfully. 'It's always been my chief professional enemy. Probably be a world-class plutocrat today if it wasn't for that impediment. But I can't seem to shake it off. Stand clear!'

And I raised another gnome and hurled it down onto the concrete, failing to suppress totally a faint smile at the spectacle of Chisholm leaping nimbly back a foot or two to avoid the explosion of plaster.

'Stop that, Daley!' barked the outraged sleuth.

'Very well, Mr Chisholm,' I sighed. 'What can I do for you?'

He waved a document in my face.

'I've got a search warrant, Daley. Constable Jones and I intend to search your premises.'

£A social conscience has always been my chief professional enemy

'I see. Well, if you'd care to tell me what you're looking for perhaps I could save you a gruelling and time-consuming effort.'

'But if I tell you what we're looking for, you might find some way to conceal or remove the offending item, Mr Daley. So I prefer not to. But before we start searching I'd like to hear why you've been massacring these innocent gnomes.'

'That's just it, Mr Chisholm. They is far from innocent. They is vicious, harmful gnomes. I have had a complaint from a customer that her little boy broke one accidentally and cut himself on a sharp edge that was left over. Had to have seven stitches in hospital.'

'Kindly show me the complaint, Daley.'

'It was a telephone complaint, Mr Chisholm. Anonymous. Caller didn't want no bother – just to warn me I was selling potentially dangerous gnomes. So I felt I had no option but to smash them all up just in case one of them should get into the hands of another tender, innocent child somewhere.'

'Very public-spirited, Daley,' sighed Chisholm. 'Naturally, I don't believe a word of it.'

'I'm sorry about that, Mr Chisholm.'

'So am I. Honesty is the quality I value most in a criminal. Right, we'll conduct our search.'

'Perhaps you'd like to start with the few remaining gnomes, Mr Chisholm?'

'No, thank you. I suspect the unfortunate ornaments have long since yielded up any secrets they may have contained.'

'Well, I hope you're successful in whatever it is you are looking for.'

Chisholm glared at me for a long moment with a face like the blade of a guillotine. Then he smiled and his face softened to something more like a headsman's axe.

'I don't expect to be, Mr Daley. Not this time round. I have an idea one of those unhappy gnomes might have had an interesting tale to tell but is no longer in any condition to grass. However, we'll do our duty, won't we, Jones?'

The Welsh Sherlock Holmes unlocked his gaze from a stray bird which was fluttering about the roof struts and asked:

'What's that?'

'Oh nothing vital. Sorry to have interrupted your bird watching.' Chisholm turned back to me. 'Yes, we'll do our duty, Arthur Daley, as the warrant entitles us to. And then we'll leave you to get on with your life and crimes. But we'll be back. I promise you that. We'll come back with another warrant and another and then another after that. And one fine day, in some secret nook or cranny, one find day, Arthur Daley, I'll find the evidence I need to put you away.'

And as the two cops began to turn over my lovely lock-up I no longer felt the smallest impulse to gloat at having put one over on them. Indeed, as I raised yet another grinning gnome only to smash its plaster body to the ground, dark and sombre forebodings were claiming me for their own.

CHAPTER SIX

FAIR SHARES

THINK BIG, YES. But also play it by the book. Of course, to do that, you need to know what's in the book. And I freely admit that I have never had much time for reading and heavy study. I am a man of action, a busy entrepreneur engrossed in commercial undertakings, and not a bookworm mugging over musty old books of law in some gloomy library. Trouble was, I had a sleuth dogging my footsteps and getting so close I could feel his hot breath on the back of my neck. If I'd just had a little more time I could certainly have rescued the flotation and gone public. As it was I very nearly came to grief. And all through being far too honest for the wicked times in which we live.

It began when I saw the Ferushi coming in through the gates of my car lot. I was a bit surprised because it was not banging and jetting out blue smoke as it had been doing when I had last seen it in what passed for running order with that machine. That had been about eighteen months before. After that the rusty old tin can had been standing out in all weathers for a year and a half until Tel had succeeded only the week before in offloading it onto some unsuspecting geezer. Or that was what I had assumed. Naturally, I also assumed, when I saw the horrible thing ease up outside my hi-tech caravan office, that the purchaser had come to kick up a fuss and demand his money back. Such obstacles to free enterprise are part of the burden borne by every entrepreneur, and I had developed a very effective technique for handling them. Adopting a bright and welcoming smile, I hurried out to greet

£ These first-class shares in Daley Enterprises will give a lifetime of satisfaction. And as a special introductory offer we are including a new transistor radio with all purchases of over a hundred pounds

the troublemaker, noting with faint surprise that he seemed a well dressed and affluent-looking bloke in his mid-forties. I had expected to see a kid in a tracksuit, possibly accompanied by a gum-chewing blonde.

'Hello, hello, hello,' I called cheerfully as I approached. 'Come to thank us for selling you this remarkable vintage automobile?'

The man smiled faintly and, as I'd anticipated, shook his head.

'Not really –' he began.

'Don't tell me. Some little problem? There's always teething troubles with these high-performance models. What is it? Steering just a tiny bit off-centre?'

'Oh no, the steering's excellent.'

'It's the clutch, isn't it? That grating noise, like a food mixer full of gravel – it's a characteristic of the Ferushi. It seems the Turkish engineers what designed –'

'The transmission is quite in order.'

'Good, good. Then it's got to be that thump from the rear? In any other car you'd be justified in assuming the differential was dicky but –'

'I've had the differential completely stripped and refurbished. It works splendidly now.'

I was a bit surprised at hearing of such expensive attention lavished on what I considered a rotten old banger. But I nodded approvingly.

'Well, naturally it always improves performance, doesn't it? Stripping and refurbishing that is. Clearly you prize the vehicle?'

'I'd have paid ten times your asking price. And considered myself lucky to have got hold of the car.'

It is at moments like these that a tycoon's mettle is tested. A mere pedlar of old rattletraps, like say Gearbox Gus in his garden shed off Tooley Street, would probably have burst into tears at hearing those words. But I slid smoothly into a routine that I had devised long ago for coping with just such agonising situations. Ducking my head, as if to avoid spattering the customer, I started to cough fiercely. The point of this was to conceal the likely fact that I had turned a little pale at this appalling news. It also provided time for me to do a lightning calculation in my quick brain which revealed that, if Tel had done his valuation properly, I would have made seven thousand five hundred sovs on my initial investment of two hundred. Having established this melancholy fact, I continued coughing for a moment longer to give me time to come up with a plan for rescuing the loot – that is the situation. But, quick as my wits undoubtedly are, the challenge was simply too sudden and I could not concoct anything very useful.

The Chairman,
Daley Enterprises

'Sorry about that,' I gasped, as I mopped my streaming eyes. 'Always catches up with me this time of year – the hay fever. Shocking, I call it. We can put Yanks on the moon and we can't find a cure for a bit of pollen blowing about in the air. Now as regards the Ferushi, it is, of course, possible that my assistant got the price wrong. If you'll hang on a mo I'll just pop into the office and see if I can find our list so –'

'This one?'

He had withdrawn from his breast pocket our current price-list and was holding it up. I nodded faintly. He said firmly:

'The price was quite right – seven hundred and fifty pounds. Incredible value for an '81 Ferushi. One of them changed hands in Aberdeen last week for fifteen thousand.'

'Really?' I gasped. 'Well, we pride ourselves, unlike some of the wheeler dealers with a patch of gravel and a row of clapped-out old bangers bear-

ing ridiculous price tags that disgrace Fulham, on being both connoisseurs and honest dealers. May I ask, why have you gratified us with a return visit? Could it be to tender your undying gratitude?'

'Yes, in part. I really needed a Ferushi for my collection. I'm a vintage and rare car freak amongst other things, you see. But I also looked in to enquire if you might have anything else that would interest me?'

I did a lightning mental survey of our current stock. Nothing remotely suitable came to mind but it is my firm policy never to disappoint a customer so I said enticingly:

'What would you say to a '52 Ferrari – er – Carissima?'

'Carissima? That's a new one on me.'

'No need to be embarrassed. Very few collectors have ever heard of it. They only made three altogether.'

'Really? Could I have a look at it?'

'Certainly. Of course. Not today, naturally, since it's in our special secure store somewhere in Wiltshire. It's in its original state and would need – like you said – stripping and refurbishing. And I'm not absolutely certain it's still got its original Carissima badge but I could have one –'

'Actually,' he interrupted courteously, 'now that I come to think of it, I don't really need another Ferrari at this stage. I have seven in my collection. Anything else?'

'Indeed there is. What would you say to a very fascinating Ford Zodiac from the fifties with –'

He shook his head with a touch of impatience.

'No, no – I'm talking about collector's items.'

'Ah – them. Yes – well – they're a bit thin in the lot just at present but I'll tell you what. If you leave me your phone number I'll give you a bell just as soon as the next one comes in. And I

think I can promise you that it won't be long before
one does.'

'All right. I've got a card here somewhere –'

He began rummaging in a bulging wallet which
contained, I noticed, enough plastic to deal a poker
hand from. As he searched he talked amiably.

'I can't help feeling I've heard your name
before, Mr Daley. Are you exclusively a car dealer?
Or do you have other business interests?'

I laughed in a politely incredulous way.

'Me? Do I have other interests? I think it's fair
to say, Mr – er –'

'Carboy. Selwyn Carboy.'

'Not – not Carboy of Carboy Homebuilder?'

'Yes. That's me.'

'Well, it's certainly a pleasure to meet you,
Mr Carboy. I've long been an admirer of your
business empire. I have to admit that I'm not
quite in your league yet – although I am one of
the most substantial entrepreneurs in Fulham with
several flourishing companies under my control.'

'Ah, here's my card.' He handed it to me.
'Would you be offended if I offered some advice,
Mr Daley?'

'Honoured, more like it.'

'Go public.'

'Do what?'

'It's amazing what a difference it makes. I was
like you seven or eight years ago – dabbling in
this and that – doing quite well financially but
somehow not really in the top league. And then
I went public.'

'I see. And – er – where exactly did this take
place, Mr Carboy?'

'Well, on the exchange, naturally. I strongly
advise you to make a flotation. And I'll tell you
what – after benefiting from your honesty in the
matter of the Ferushi, I'd certainly consider taking

a few shares off your hands.'

'Really? Well, that's – that's jolly decent of you, Mr Carboy. Shares, you say?'

'Yes, of the public company. If you take my advice and make the flotation.'

'Would that be in addition to going public?'

'Pretty much the same thing, wouldn't you say?'

'Yes. Now that you mention it – very much the same. Well, you've certainly given me food for thought.'

'Good. And don't forget to give me a buzz if anything in the vintage car line turns up.'

'I won't. Never fear.'

'Goodbye then.'

And with a friendly wave, he got back into the misshapen Ferushi and was soon purring smoothly out of the lot.

Even as I sent a last little salute after him, I was groping in my pocket for my ignition key. And minutes later I was humming through Fulham in a vehicle much closer to being suitable transport for a prince of commerce than the hideous Ferushi, that is my superb twelve-cylinder Jaguar saloon. And a few minutes after that I was pounding on the front door of the curious structure – a cross between a conservatory and a dustbin shed – which Terence McCann called home. Of course, I could have phoned but we went back a long way did Tel and I. We knew each other down to the smallest tremor in the voice. So I was aware that, no matter how I tried to hide it, Terry would know at once from my tone that I was labouring under deep emotion. And I didn't want him forewarned. I wanted him to get the full force of my fury unprepared.

'Open up before I beat the door down, you pillock!' I thundered, as I pounded for the third or fourth time on his glass-panelled front door.

I knew he was inside because he was dating a new girl and had taken her out to lunch for the first time. Since I had nothing special for him to do in the afternoon and since I am, I think I can with modesty proclaim, a model employer I had given him permission to be a little late back from lunch if a favourable opportunity presented itself for him to become better-acquainted with the young lady. True, I was not unaware that the girl's father owned three carpet shops in and around Fulham and could thus prove a valuable business contact once more as he had been in the past before a commercial disagreement had come between us.

'I know you're in there,' I called. 'I can see suggestive shadows through the frosted glass. And I warn you, if you don't open the door –'

''Ere, what are you? Some kind of kinky old bugger?' asked a lovely girl, lightly dressed, flinging open the door and addressing me in loud, shrill Cockney.

For a moment I goggled at her and, since I am always the perfect gentleman, tried to prevent my goggle from slipping down from her face to the large part of her pretty figure which was visible. This because she was clad in nothing more concealing than a half-cup bra and net knickers.

'Certainly not, my dear,' I informed her politely. 'My name is Arthur Daley and I have reason to suspect that Terry McCann is in there somewhere. I would like a word with him.'

'Well, you can't,' she responded crossly. ''E ain't got no clothes on.'

I blinked in renewed surprise at her accent. Why did it affect me like that? Because the girl was Japanese and it was strange to hear the age-old tones of South London issuing from her delicate Oriental lips.

'Then perhaps,' I suggested, 'you'd convey my

respects and request him politely to slip into his dressing gown so that – oh, there you are!'

Behind the girl, a door, which I knew led to the chamber of horrors that Tel called his bed-room, had opened and the master of the house, dressing-gown pulled hastily about him, emerged with a grim expression.

'What the hell you doing here?' was his churlish greeting.

'All in good time. May I step into your par-lour?'

'No, you bloody well can't!' responded the Japanese bimbo who apparently combined the appearance of an Oriental angel with the tem-perament of a South London harpy. 'Tell him to piss off, Tel!'

'You shouldn't be here, Arthur,' Terry more moderately suggested. 'We had an agreement.'

'If you'll just forgive me, my dear,' I said, doffing my cap as I edged past the glorious, but aggressive, damsel into what passes for Terry's living room. 'I just thought I should inform you without delay, Terence, that I am in shtook for seven and a half big bills because of your bungling. And I intend to dock you half your weekly salary every week until they is paid back.'

'What weekly salary?' he sneered.

'Two hundred sovs a week.'

'You don't pay me two hundred sovs a week.'

'It's a notional figure. Which yields a notional one hundred sovs a week as half of it. And that is the sum I intend to reclaim from you until the debt is paid off.'

'What the hell you talking about?'

'You let that priceless vintage car go for pea-nuts. You're supposed to do the valuations on all purchases, aren't you?'

'So?'

'So why did you let that magnificent Ferushi escape for just one tenth of its true value?'

He gazed at me in such astonishment that I found myself momentarily feeling sorry for the baffled chap. But it is my firm policy, like those of the many of the great figures in the history of tycoonery, never to yield to sentimental feelings when there is a sov to be picked up by standing firm. So I said gently but firmly:

'Since we has known each other a long time, Terence, I will do my best to reject the obvious explanation, which is that you and Carboy put together a little scam to defraud me of the vehicle's true value. I therefore won't accuse you of getting a kickback from the enormous saving he made on the purchase.'

'What purchase? What you on about?'

'I suspect you know very well but I have no objection to refreshing your memory.'

And that's what I did, starting from the day, a year and a half ago, when Terence had entered the yard at the wheel of the Ferushi. It was then progressing in short jerks, as if jet-propelled by

'Terence, I am in shtook for seven and a half big bills because of your bungling'

its repeated back-firing. After spending a couple of hours contemplating its bottom, Tel had pinned a price tag to its windscreen offering the wreck for a thousand sovs. After nine months with no takers, he had reduced the outrageous demand to seven fifty. And that was the price at which Carboy had acquired it.

While I was going through this history, Kura Evans first stormed about the room in her bra and knickers, uttering fierce oaths, and then retired to the bedroom from which, now and then, issued screams of abuse at me mingled with exhortations to Terry to 'come to bed, Tel, I only got another hour!' At some point before she left the room Terence had muttered a surly introduction and from this I had learned her name and concluded that she must be only half Japanese since 'Evans' is presumably not a particularly common surname in the land of the rising sun.

'So tough,' grunted Terry when I had finished my unhappy story.

'Very tough. With that seven and a half grand I could have embarked on my overdue modernisation programme. As it is all I'll get is a hundred a week from you, which is just a trickle of small practical value.'

'In that case, don't bother with it.'

'Then how you gonna clear the debt, Tel?'

'Would you consider accepting a vodka and slimline as full settlement when I see you down the Winchester this evening?'

'This is no joking matter.'

'Then stop making comical remarks. I never come on as no used car expert. So you'll just have to write it off to experience.'

At this point a dismal sound, a bit like a mother wolf baying for one of her cubs what had got lost in the snows, came from the bedroom.

'Does she always howl like that?' I asked, unable to suppress a faint shudder.

'How would I know? First time I been alone with her. Except that you're here so I'm not alone with her, am I? So on your bike, Arthur.'

'Listen, Tel, all may not be lost. I got a plan.'

'Good. I don't want to hear it.'

'What would you say if I went public?'

'I'd say it was great if you went anywhere.'

'I'm talking about a flotation, Tel.'

'Lovely. Have fun on the river.' He raised his voice. 'Coming, darling.'

'You don't understand, do you?'

'No.'

'That's because you're ignorant of high finance. The point is I'm thinking of flogging shares. And that could be a way out for you.'

'I'd rather it was a way out for you.'

'I admit it's hard to talk business with that she-devil blowing a gasket in the bedroom. But consider this: if you was to get' – I lowered my voice discreetly – 'her father to take a parcel of shares, I'd knock the value of them off the money you owe me. He's got three carpet shops. Seven and a half grand's worth of shares would be nothing to him. And it would put you in the clear.'

At this point such a shriek of rage and anguish came spiralling out of the bedroom that both Tel and I jumped to our feet. I urged:

''Ere, you'd better get in there before she turns into butter or something. We'll talk about it some more tonight. But remember, get her father in the right mood – something like what she's in at present – and flog him the shares.'

With which I offered Tel an encouraging smile and tiptoed away, leaving him gazing after me with a puzzled expression.

'What do you know about share flotations,

'Where did you learn all that, Dave?' I asked in amazement

Dave?' I asked as I sipped my first voddy and
slimline of the evening in the Winchester while
waiting for Tel to show.

I had put the question more for the joy of
watching a look of incomprehension steal across
Dave's face than in the hope of getting an answer.
This look, a classic, could be produced by questions
no more challenging than: 'What language do they
speak in France?' or 'Is London north or south of
Edinburgh?'

*'Hello, is that the
financial editor?'*

'Share flotations?' murmured Dave, apparently
trying to extract inspiration from the words. But
the next moment he showed that he didn't need
any for he went on: 'They is the process by which
a private company becomes a public company. It
does this by offering its shares on the open market
at a predetermined price which it estimates is the
value of the company. These shares then rise and
fall in value according to the confidence what the
public has in them. They is quoted on the stock
exchange and listed in the financial sections of the
papers.'

I gazed at him in amazement.

'Where you learn all that, Dave?'

'From Bonzo Hooper, who used to own this
place. Gave me my first job as barman. Flogged
it to me at a rock-bottom price when he emigrated
to Chile and I'd saved up enough.'

'Yeah, I remember Bonzo. But why did he
teach you about high finance?'

'He was really teaching himself, Arthur. He
wanted to be an accountant. He used to make
me hear him answer questions from his books.
But he didn't have a very good brain. He kept
failing his exams and so I had to go on helping
him for years. Some of the stuff just stuck in my
mind I suppose.'

'So how would I set about floating my company,
Dave?'

He gazed at me with faint reproach.

'How should I know, Arthur?'

And, of course, I then realised that he'd just been reeling the stuff off from memory and didn't really understand the first thing about it.

A week or so later, I picked up the phone and dialled the number of a posh national newspaper. When the voice answered, I said:

'Financial editor, please.'

'One moment.'

It had been a busy week. But now the flotation was almost complete. One million pounds' worth of one-pound shares in Daley Enterprises were soon going to hit the market. In fact, five thousand of them had already been sold. To my delight and astonishment, Terry had actually succeeded in flogging them to William Evans, father of the furious Kura, an ex-sheep farmer who had been in the carpet business for a quarter of a century and was married to a Japanese lady.

'Yes?'

'Hello, is that the financial editor?'

'It is.'

'Arthur Daley here.'

'I see.'

'I think you may be interested to hear that I'm floating shares in my company, Daley Enterprises.'

'Who's handling it?'

'Sorry?'

'Who's handling the flotation?'

'Like I said, I am.'

'No, no, which merchant bank?'

'No merchant bank. I'm a firm believer in self-help. I remain a good Thatcherite even though that wise and perceptive lady no longer holds sway over the destiny of this great nation and –'

'Yes, all right, but what about this flotation?

What's the name of your company again?'

'Daley Enterprises.'

'No, I've never heard of it.'

'You will. At present we're just getting into our stride. What I'm phoning about is the share price. We're kicking off at a quid a share. So I'd like to know the drill: do I phone you every day? And if so, what time would you prefer?'

'I'm sorry I don't understand. Phone me about what?'

'Well, the share price, of course. I'm thinking of just putting it up by a modest ten p a day. Tell you what, why don't you just add that – ten p – every day until I tell you something different. Save a lot of unnecessary phoning, wouldn't it?'

'Is this some kind of joke?'

'No, of course not. You list all share prices, don't you?'

At this point, I saw, through the window, Terry's old banger draw up and then the man himself, looking troubled, emerge and head swiftly towards me. The voice on the phone said:

'Yes, we publish closing prices.'

'Well then – could you please add my closing prices to the list?'

'I don't understand. When it gets quoted on the exchange we'll print it automatically.'

I laughed in a friendly way.

'Oh, it's that way round is it? Muggins here was under the impression you printed the price and then the exchange got hold of the good news later.'

There was an indistinct sound through the phone.

'Look, I really don't need this. Tokyo's in turmoil. Wall Street is boiling over. Save the gags for another day, would you, PLEASE!'

And the phone went dead. I was about to phone

the bloke back and remonstrate when the door flew open and Terry, looking something like a fugitive from a chain gang, strode in.

'They've been following me,' he announced grimly.

'Who has?'

'Chisholm and Jones. What's more they wasn't doing it openly in their car. They was sneaking round corners and hiding behind pillar boxes. I wouldn't have spotted them if I hadn't caught a glimpse of their ugly mugs in the mirror behind the bar.'

'What bar? You been in a pub?'

'For half an hour – just long enough to gulp a lager and munch a Scotch egg. I'm entitled to that, ain't I?'

'Yeah, yeah – keep your strength up. Have you considered that maybe Chisholm was just passing by?'

'Well if he was it's uncanny how our paths kept crossing. I kept my eye out after I left the Duck and Kettle and that's when I saw him and Jones doing the John le Carré bit.'

'You weren't doing nothing dodgy, were you?'

'I dunno. I was putting your hooky prospectuses in letter boxes like you told me.'

'Perfectly legit. In fact, it's compulsory. It said in my book on business practice that when you go public it's necessary to issue a prospectus. Well, that's what we're doing.'

Terry opened his briefcase and upended it on my desk. A cascade of plain brown envelopes tumbled out.

'Well from now I'd prefer it if you got someone else to hand out your junk mail.'

'Tel, what is this? I've already crossed off your debt because of the success of the scheme.'

'What success? Evans only bought those shares

'They've been following me,' he announced grimly

because he wants me to marry Kura, which no sane man would. Anyway they isn't shares. They is just pieces of coloured paper we had run off down the duplicator shop.'

'Steady on. We modelled them on a proper share certificate. Fingers Docherty nicked it from a stockbroker's office.'

'Arthur, the fact is you don't know nothing about city-level finance. What you think you flogged Evans is just mickey mouse shares.'

'Never. We done it by the book. We've printed a prospectus. We've printed the share certificates and we're getting them listed in the paper. Only –'

'Only what?'

'No, it's just that – I was on the dog to a city editor a little while ago. I wanted to get him to quote our shares and –'

I found myself licking my lips slightly.

'And what?'

'It's just that he asked which merchant bank was handling the flotation.'

Terry slapped the desk top.

'That's it. It's not something you're allowed to do DIY. You're in shtook, Arthur.'

'Okay, okay – look, hand me the yellow pages, would you?'

'Why?' Terry asked, doing so. 'What you want them for?'

'Find the number of the nearest merchant bank. There must be some in Fulham.'

'Here, what exactly does a merchant bank do?'

'Do? Funny, don't seem to be none. It's – er – well, it's a bank for merchants, isn't it?'

'You've already got one of those.'

'I know but – my bank doesn't do flotations. That's what merchant banks mainly do – flotations. 'Ere, there's not a single one listed in the yellow pages. So how the hell do you get onto them?'

I managed it in the end but only after much asking about. The place was called Denzil Walzheimer and it was located in the City of London. I phoned and, with some difficulty, secured an appointment for the following week. It was with someone called Carboni who, it seemed, was head of a department called corporate finance. I told his secretary on the phone that I needed to see him about an urgent matter connected with a flotation and she was quite helpful. She said that normally he was booked up for two to three months in advance but he'd make an exception for a possible new client. I began to think Terry might have been right in suggesting there was more to this flotation business than I'd thought. I told the girl I'd probably only need about an hour of the bloke's time in the first place and I assumed that it wouldn't involve a huge fee. She said, oh no, the fee for a preliminary consultation would be minimal.

I asked, 'What – around a tenner?'

She laughed in a well-bred voice and said, 'Oh, very amusing.'

'More than that?'

'Well, just a bit. Mr Carboni's minimum fee is one hundred and fifty pounds an hour.'

I told her I was glad she had appreciated my little joke even as I reached for the vodka bottle.

She said, 'Does the appointment stand?'

'Oh, definitely,' I said. 'I'm just baffled at how reasonable it is.'

Sitting a week later in Mr Carboni's outer office, which was considerably smaller than Euston Station, I began to realise why some people think the City of London does itself a bit too well. The whole atmosphere of Denzil Walzheimer was one of wealth and luxury. In the corridor I'd actually passed a butler in full buttling gear. Okay it was

Getting ready to float Daley Enterprises

pricey, but with a bloke like Carboni spearheading my application I was sure the flotation would at last get flotating. Within a year or so I might even have an outer office like this one and, if I was ever stuck for readies, could rent it out for a day or two as indoor tennis courts.

'Mr Carboni will see you now, Mr Daley. If you'd like to follow me –'

She had oozed in without a sound, a process helped by the carpets which was deep enough to hide nesting pheasants. I rose and followed her. Mr Carboni's office itself was not immense but cosy with lots of leather and wood. There was quite a few books on the walls and a big painting of a girl with a face that looked as if it had been sliced into odd-shaped strips which had then been carelessly reassembled but which somehow managed to suggest that it was worth a fortune.

Carboni himself was a thin, bespectacled man in his mid-thirties with a bright, but not exactly warm, smile. He was examining a document as we entered but quickly put it down and came round his desk with hand extended.

'Mr Daley? Delighted to meet you. Shall we sit over here? Less officey.'

He led me to two deep leather chairs facing a marble-topped table.

'A drink? Coffee?'

Reflecting that each time I paused for a sip the meter would clock up a tenner or so I declined refreshment. The secretary withdrew. Carboni began without ceremony.

'So you want to go public?'

'I think the time could be ripe for it, yes.'

'May I ask why?'

'Well, you know, raise capital for expansion and suchlike.'

'Of course. Now what is your present turnover?'

'Oh, I leave all that side of it to my accountant. I mean, I'm too busy thinking up fresh initiatives to spend my life poring over figures.'

'I understand. But it is within the stock market guidelines?'

'Not much doubt about that.'

'That's around ten million at present. Of course they prefer a more substantial figure but we could probably get listing on ten million. What kind of breakdown do you envisage?'

'No, no breakdown. I plan to just keep steaming along.'

'No, I meant what type of shares are you thinking of issuing?'

'Oh just the usual kind. Nothing fancy although I have got a weakness for the ones with coloured pictures on them. Maybe showing the face of my great heroine, Margaret Thatcher, surrounded by naked little boys blowing trumpets. But I'd probably leave that to you people.'

'Erm, Mr Daley, I was asking what proportion

of preference shares to ordinary shares and, of course, how many of the A and B kinds?'

'Couldn't you deal with details like that?'

'Well naturally we would advise you. But first we'll really have to get a clearer picture of your asset profile.'

'Probably got one somewhere in my office but I didn't think to bring it. However, I did bring this.'

I took from my inside pocket a copy of our prospectus. Carboni raised an eyebrow slightly.

'And what would that be?'

'It's our prospectus.'

'Oh, you've drafted some suggestions, have you? Very enterprising. Not many of our customers do.'

My great heroine, Margaret Thatcher

He opened the envelope and began to read, murmuring the words aloud as he did so.

'These first-class shares in Daley Enterprises will give a lifetime of satisfaction. And as a special introductory offer we are including a new transistor radio with all purchases of over a hundred pounds –' with a frown Carboni looked up at me. 'Mr Daley, what exactly is this document?'

'Well, it's – er – it's my brother's.'

'Your brother's?'

'I'll come clean, Mr Carboni. You've probably realised by now that I'm not here on my own behalf. No, I'm quite happy for the present with my own flourishing business and my prominent position in Fulham business circles. But my brother is getting out of hand.'

'I don't understand.'

'He gets these delusions of grandeur, imagines he's one of the Gettys or the Rockingfellows. He's been treated for it. Normally it's just a harmless eccentricity but it's been brought to my attention that he's started acting out his fantasies. He's been putting that prospectus through letter boxes and trying to sell people shares what he's had printed himself. He even phoned up a newspaper editor and asked him to put the price of his mickey mouse shares in the paper. Now, what I'd like you to tell me is – has my brother been doing anything illegal?'

'Well, it certainly sounds like it, yes.'

'What exactly.'

'Well, it's hard to know where to begin.'

Carboni rose and went to a nearby bookshelf from which he took down a fat, official-looking volume with a leather binding. He turned through it confidently and soon found the place he was looking for.

'Yes, here's the section: "No person other than an authorised person can issue or cause to be issued an investment advertisement in the UK unless its contents have been approved . . ." Well, there you are. That would take in this childish parody of an offer document. And, technically speaking, I fear it's probable that your deluded brother has committed a whole range of other offences.'

'And would these be serious offences?'

'Oh very. In principle.'

'Locking-up offences?'

'All financial fraud carries severe penalties. But I really don't think you need worry unduly, Mr Daley.'

'Why not?'

'Because what you've shown me is clearly not intended to be taken seriously. It's more like a child playing Monopoly than real finance. No, the only way in which your brother could be in trouble would be if he'd taken money in the course of his activities.'

I felt a tight sensation at the back of my throat.

£ I could see I was involved in the most ludicrous financial operation since the Sundance Kid and that other one blew up the train full of money

'Money?'

'Yes, if he'd had the misfortune to come across someone gullible or ill-informed enough to take him seriously and actually handed over some money for his toytown shares. Then I imagine the courts would have to take a serious view of your poor brother's – Mr Daley? I say – Where are you off to? Mr Daley?'

'Just remembered. Vital engagement. Be in touch soon when I'm ready for my own flotation. And my cheque will be in the post. Thanks for the advice.'

And I hastened out of his office.

I hot-wheeled it back to Fulham and straight to Terry's garden hut. There I beat on the door for some time. But I could get no response. So I went round the back and, by peering through a crack in the curtains, established that Terry was not entertaining Kura or some other eager lady that afternoon. In which case he was probably at the lock-up. I had to get to him before Chisholm did. Then maybe we could figure out some way of paying Evans his money back and avoiding being banged up for the rest of our naturals for fraud.

I hurried back to the front of the quaint residence and, as I rounded the corner, came to a dead stop and quickly went into reverse. But I was not fast enough.

'Well, well, Arthur Daley. Come to cook up some new villainy with your partner in crime?'

'Oh, hello, Mr Chisholm. I appreciate a police officer with a sense of humour. Was you looking for Terry then?'

'I was as it happened. We think we've got him bang to rights, don't we, Jones?'

The moon-faced Welsh sleuth was, at that moment, scratching his right hip and gazing absently at a row of starlings on a small tree in

Terry's garden.

'Jones,' Chisholm repeated with a hint of reproach in his voice.

'Hm? Oh, that's right, Sarge,' he agreed.

Chisholm sighed.

'Jones, you are not yet famous enough for *Spitting Image*. So is it necessary for you to act like a latex doll?'

'Sorry, Sarge. Why don't we just go in and nab McCann?'

'Admirable idea, Jones. But for its implementation, we must locate the felon first. Could I therefore prevail upon you to step round to the back and see if he's there?'

'He's not,' I said quickly.

'And you would, of course, be scrupulously truthful about that, would you not, Mr Daley?'

'Absolutely. Because, you see, I don't think you've got a case.'

'Really? You know all about the trouble he's in then?'

I heaved what I hoped was an invisible sigh of relief. Clearly the two rozzers did not yet know of my own involvement in the possible fraud. I asked:

'Am I correct in thinking that you want to give Terry a hard time about some money he owes?'

'That's one way of putting it.'

'And that because of this money he has, in your estimate, been guilty of something very like fraud?'

'Very like it indeed, Mr Daley.'

'Well, the heat's off, Sergeant. Because you see I'm going to pay it for him. The truth is, Terry is not to blame for what he's done because he's in an unstable mental condition – stress brought on by dating a female tiger and – no court in the land would convict. Any shrink would testify that he's –'

Terry came swinging down the path towards us. I shouted, 'Terry. It's okay. I'm fixing it. Don't run. Most you'll get is a suspended sentence.'

'What you talking about?' asked Terry, halting as he reached us.

'They has come to arrest you, Tel,' I said gently. 'And you has certainly been a naughty lad. But I know it's all because of the girl –'

'What girl?' asked Terry.

'Yes, what girl?' asked Sergeant Chisholm.

'Beautiful, she is. As so many of them are, don't you think, Sergeant? That is the children of two races in whom the beauty of the West combines with the grace of the East. I'm talking about Kura Evans. Terry only did it because she spurned his advances. He was distracted, disconsolate, totally shattered and so he dreamed up this share scheme just to get even with her old man. You see he thought – didn't you, Tel? – that her dad had forbidden her from seeing him. So he conned the old Taffy out of five grand. He wanted me to join him in it. He was raving, saying we could make millions from flogging his mickey mouse shares. But of course I refused to have anything to do with it. And I was horrified when I saw he'd printed his childish share certificates in the name of Daley Enterprises.'

Terry stared at me in amazement.

'What you trying to do to me, Arthur?'

'Settle out of court, Tel,' I urged, smuggling a quick wink past the watching coppers. 'And I'm prepared to put up the cash to do so. So all we need is to persuade old man Evans to accept his money back. I'll write out a cheque this very moment.'

With a flourish I got out my cheque book.

'No, you won't,' snapped Chisholm, pushing my hand down again. 'Not with possible charges

This is where Terry's mickey mouse shares were definitely NOT traded

pending. Evans, you say? Japanese daughter? That's the carpet shop Evans, isn't it? Come along, Mr McCann. We'll all just drive round to his office and have a word with Mr Evans.'

'I've done nothing –' began Terry heatedly.

But I hushed him with finger to lips.

'Better stay shtum, Tel. As soon as you've left with them I'll get straight on the dog to my brief. So go with Sergeant Chisholm peacefully, my son. Believe me, flying fists would be folly at this stage.'

Terry stared at me in disbelief for a moment. Then his eyes contracted into contempt.

'This is pretty slimy even for you, isn't it, Arthur?'

'You see?' I invited Chisholm. 'He attacks his benefactor. The boy's completely disoriented. Even if Evans won't take his money back he'll get off on an insanity plea.'

Terry shook his head.

'It's no go, Arthur. I'm going to tell –'

'Terence!' I said urgently, giving him the faint nod. 'Believe me. This is the best way.'

We gazed at each other for a long moment. Then Tel shrugged very slightly. He turned to Chisholm and held out his hands.

'Cuffs?' he asked ironically.

'Oh, I don't think that will be necessary, McCann,' said Chisholm benignly. 'I doubt if you'll go for a facelift and a flight to Buenos Aires. Besides Jones is a powerful man, aren't you, Jones?'

The constable was gazing straight at his chief with a patient smile on his face but he failed to respond. Chisholm sighed.

'I sometimes wonder, Jones, if you're under some kind of spell. Did you hear what I said?'

'Said? When, Sarge?'

'Just before Merlin waved his wand at you. Do you think you can still drive, Jones? Or would you prefer to take us all on your broomstick?'

A moment or two later the three of them disappeared up the path and I leaned against a tree and mopped my brow.

'But why the hell didn't you tell me?' I asked Terry for the third or fourth time when, about three hours later, he returned from the cop shop.

'Because you'd have had a heart attack.'

'What you talking about?'

'Finding out I'd given back five big ones. 'Course you would. Blimey, Arthur, I've seen you gasp and clutch your side after misplacing a tenner.'

I gave him the long, suspicious glance.

'So you did it all for me? You was just thinking of my legal well-being?'

''Course not. I was thinking of my legal well-being. I could see I was involved in the most ludicrous financial operation since the Sundance Kid and that other one blew up a train full of money. I didn't want any part in it. But I have to say that I was also thinking of you. Believe it or not – and just now after having been grilled by that sarcastic little ferret for three hours I think I must have been crazy – I quite often try to keep you out of trouble.'

'So instead of banking the cheque like I'd instructed you, you just buzzed along to Evans and asked him to take it back?'

'No. He'd have smelled a rat and maybe sent for Chisholm. Evans has no love for you, Arthur, especially since you sold him all that hooky Axminster a couple years back. So I got Kura to remove the stub from his cheque book and I just tore up the cheque. He never even remembered he bought those shares when Chisholm came down on him about it.'

'I could sue you. You realise that?'

'Fine, sue away. Ask Evans for the cheque back and then bring an action from Parkhurst or wherever they puts you.'

'Yeah well –'

'You were quite prepared to dump me in it.'

'It seemed the best strategy for both of us. How was I to know they was only after you for not showing a road tax disk?'

'Anyway, won't do us any good. Chisholm'll be hotter than ever after having been – as he'll see it – made a fool of.'

'We got to get him off our backs somehow. What the hell's that?'

I slid to the floor as a series of sharp reports came from just outside the caravan.

'Get down on the floor like me, Tel,' I urged. 'It's either the Old Bill storming us or some gangster what you've offended.'

'It's the Ferushi,' said Terry, gazing out of the window.

'The what?'

'The Turkish car. It's back-firing again. Moreover it looks like quite a few bits and pieces have fallen off it. The owner don't look too cheerful this time round.'

I stood up and headed for the caravan's back door which I had had expensively installed for just such emergencies as this one.

'You talk to him, Tel,' I said, pulling it open. 'You sold him that heap of rolling scrap-iron in the first place. I've got a meet with someone at the lock-up.'

''Ang about –'

But I was down the steps and sprinting for my Jaguar before the Ferushi, once again back-firing and belching out blue smoke, had pulled up outside the caravan.

CHAPTER SEVEN
THERE'S NO BUSINESS LIKE–

TERRY AND I was just stacking the last of the chairs and putting them in cardboard boxes ready to take out to the Bedford van when a pretty girl said:

'Shhh!'

'What?' I asked.

She pointed towards the stage on which a big man wearing a bedsheet was kneeling in front of a woman wearing a blue gown and sitting on a cube of painted wood.

'Please be quiet,' the girl said a bit snottily.

'We got to get these chairs shifted, my dear.'

'Please. Just be quiet for a few minutes. It's one of Bats's big scenes and he's been having a spot of trouble with it.'

'Very well.'

Tel and I stopped stacking chairs and watched what was going on. The big man gulped in a strangled kind of way and said:

'You are my true and faithful wife, as dear to me as the ruddy drops that visit my sad heart.'

Of course, I have always known a great deal of Shakespeare but I freely admit that I did not know that particular passage from the Bard's powerful play, *Julius Caesar*, until I became involved with the production. The big man and the woman went on a bit and then a bloke wearing jeans and standing at the back of the auditorium called:

'Much better, Bats. Perhaps not quite so much sniffing and snuffling. Makes you sound a bit like a pet labrador. And Stell, darling, you're still not giving it quite enough projection. Never hear you

£ *I reckon I must have a poet's nature. Shakespeare never fails to bring tears to my eyes*

at the back here. All right, let's take ten.'

The girl who had silenced us said curtly:

'Right. You can take the rest of the chairs now.'

She drifted away and I said to Tel:

'That big bloke – actor – know him from somewhere.'

Tel grinned.

'Right. And you don't want to know him any better if you can help it.'

'Oh? Who is he then? Inland Revenue?'

Sir Laurence Guilgood

'Worse. He's someone you've stood quaking in front of once or twice. Looks different as a Roman, doesn't he? It's the Chief Super.'

I gaped at him.

'What – you mean –? Yeah, you're right, they called him Bats didn't they? Short for Batty which is short for Batty Basildon which I happen to know was the nickname he had when he went to Winchester public school. So the bloodhound of Fulham dabbles in amateur dramatics, does he?'

'Looks like it. Come on, let's get the rest of these in the van. I want to get away early tonight.'

'Date, is it?'

'With a very attractive greyhound. Mick Simmons and I are going to the dogs.'

Twenty minutes later, an unmarked car swerved round the Bedford, bowling merrily along at sixty or so, and pulled up sharp. I only just managed to brake in time.

'What the hell is – oh no!'

The groan had been wrung from me by the sight of what was descending from the car. It was a man in a civilian suit who looked more like a uniformed policeman than a uniformed policeman. He had a sharp, ferrety face and he was directing a stare like a gimlet at our Bedford van. From the other side of the little cop car issued a moon-faced fellow with a slightly bewildered smile on his jem mace.

'What they after?' asked Terry indignantly, glancing at his watch. 'I got to meet Mick in less than an hour.'

Sergeant Chisholm – he of the ferrety face – strode purposefully towards us as I wound down my window while Constable Jones ambled after him.

'Fancy bumping into you two,' said Chisholm, performing the trick whereby he smiled from chin to just below the eyes. The minces retained the deadly glare of searchlights on a prison watchtower. 'I think you've made our day this time. What do you think, Jones?'

'Exactly what you do, Sarge,' agreed the accommodating rozzer.

'Tell them why, Jones?'

'Why what, Sarge?'

Chisholm heaved a short but deeply exasperated sigh.

'Jones, I have heard it said that during the Napoleonic wars some soldiers mastered the art of sleeping on the march. But I have never before encountered a police constable who could do the same on duty. Now think hard – where have we just come from?'

'The warehouse, Sergeant. The one on the river. Where they store all the cookers and refrigerators and stuff.'

'Right in one. And what were we doing visiting that musty old warehouse, Constable? Share the amusing tale with our friends Arthur and Terry here.'

'We were responding to a call. The manager alleged there had been a break-in and robbery.'

'Excellent, Jones. Now that you've proved that, all unsuspected, you've really been with us all the time, I'll take up the gripping yarn. Yes, we got there just after the thieves had fled. And guess what? In a blue Bedford van just like this one. So we set off in pursuit and lo – what do we find a mile up the road? You and Terence McCann breezing along in this blue Bedford van. Been down by the river, have we?'

I sighed.

'No, we have not, Mr Chisholm. We have been down to the Hearts of Oak Theatre to pick up a stack of chairs that we had rented out to them.'

'Quick off the mark, Arthur. The Hearts of Oak is in the right direction. Let's have a look at these chairs.'

'Knock it off!' grumbled Terry. 'I've got a date with a betting slip.'

'This is sheer harassment, Mr Chisholm,' I said sternly. 'And I intend to lodge a very serious complaint about it.'

'Noted for reference, Arthur. Remind me to tremble in my boots after we've inspected your cargo. Now, let's move it, shall we?'

We all trooped round to the back of the van and I opened the doors. Chisholm and Jones instantly seized one of the large cardboard boxes containing chairs that filled the interior of the van and tugged it to the edge of the floor. They pulled open the flaps to reveal neatly stacked chairs.

'See?' I said balefully. 'What did I tell you?'

'Chairs, Arthur. That's what you told me. And I do, in fact, behold chairs. But two questions occur to me. One, could chairs have been amongst the items taken from the Dudley Tarquin Warehouse and two, is there perhaps more valuable merchandise, such as refrigerators, stashed underneath the chairs?'

With which he began tugging the chairs out of their box and dumping them roughly in the road.

'If you damage our chairs we'll have to charge the theatre,' I said, without much hope that it would restrain the rabid rozzer.

'Charge away, Arthur. I believe the arts are flourishing in Fulham. They should be able to bear the toll.'

'But your governor might not like it,' growled Terry. 'Chief Superintendent Basildon is one of the bigwigs down the Hearts of Oak, as you probably know.'

This inspired remark produced an immediate effect. Chisholm stopped manhandling our chairs and both sleuths gaped at us with open mouths, a revolting spectacle.

'What are you getting at, McCann?' Chisholm asked.

'Only that we've just left him – acting his head off in – what was the play, Arthur?'

'It was *Julius Caesar* by William Shakespeare. And Basildon was making a speech to his wife – his pretend wife in the play. Get him on the dog, Sergeant. He'll confirm that we was there.'

Chisholm's eyes narrowed and he glanced uneasily from me to Jones.

'Jones?' he queried. 'Make any sense to you?'

The Welsh dreamer, that is, copper, nodded.

'Mr Basildon is certainly acting in *Julius Caesar*, Sergeant. I take an interest in the arts, see? We Welsh all have great souls, mainly for singing but also for the drama. I mean look at Richard Burton who came out of the valleys and became –'

'That's enough, Jones.'

Chisholm contemplated the box of chairs doubtfully for a moment longer. Then to my astonishment he bent down and started putting the chairs that he had, a moment before, flung carelessly onto the tarmac, back into their box.

'All right,' he said, squeezing out, with obvi-

No, I do not think the Bard should be barred – but he can make life very difficult

ous reluctance, a very faint smile. 'I may have made a pardonable error on this occasion. So you can proceed with your cargo of chairs, you two. But there's always tomorrow, Arthur Daley. Yes, there's always tomorrow. Come along, Jones, we've got to get after that other Bedford van.'

And the two peelers trotted back to their car and roared off with as much bravado as a Ford Escort can generate at peak acceleration.

After battening down the hatches, Terry and I got back in the cab and set off again. Before long, Terry chuckled.

'Glad you find being persecuted so amusing, Terence,' I said with a hint of bitterness.

'Yeah, but wasn't it a treat the way they both caved in at the mention of Basildon?'

'I agree that was gratifying. Even provided some small compensation for being treated like any tuppeny tea-leaves. Unhappily it was only a one-off.'

'How about,' said Terry in a wink-wink, nudge-nudge kind of voice, 'you joining the play-acting team? You could claim you was a female impersonator and maybe get to play a woman's part opposite Basildon. Then the next time Chisholm and Jones came pounding after us you could say, "Better watch it, boys, or I'll tell my boyfriend on you."'

'Not so far-fetched as you might think, Terence. You probably weren't aware that in Shakespeare's day, all women's parts was played by boys.'

'Go on. The men was all pooftahs, was they?'

'No. It was the custom, that's all. It didn't have no erotic significance. You see, what it was –'

I paused.

'Yeah? Go on.'

But I sat silent as we weaved through the traffic in the grip of a sudden blinding inspiration. Tel, who was driving, glanced at me.

'Arthur? You haven't had a stroke, have you?'

'I think that's just what I have had, Terence. A stroke of genius. And honesty compels me to say that you was the inspiration of it. I mean, what's to stop me?'

'Stop you doing what?'

'What you said. Acting with Batty Basildon?'

'Well, I hate to be the one to tell you, Arthur, but you're not really the Marilyn Monroe type. Course, maybe with a blonde wig –'

'All right, all right, very hilarious. But just put your mind to this problem for a moment or two. Can you think of any way at all we can keep Chisholm from harassing us day and night?'

'Not offhand, no.'

'But suppose we had a powerful friend down the cop shop, one that Chisholm had to bow and scrape to? That would do it, wouldn't it?'

'What, Basildon?'

'It's possible. There's no better way to make friends than to act with them. You see, Terry, a very powerful bond of loyalty and comradeship is generated in these amateur dramatic groups.'

'How would you know?'

'I would know because many years ago I kept company with a girl who used to perform in one. So I got to know the set-up, didn't I?'

Terry said doubtfully:

'Yeah, maybe, but to get in you got to be able to act, haven't you?'

'So? I was in the school pantomime. Played one of the three little pigs. Go on, roll about. But it means I do know what it's like to tread the boards and besides I have always taken a keen interest in the drama. Only last year, I took 'er indoors up West to see *The Sound of Music*. If I set my mind to it, I have no doubt I could act most of them

Not in the Daley league, perhaps, but a success story nonetheless

bored housewives and self-fancying young men off the stage.'

'You serious?'

'I think, Terence, that our long history of being harassed by a demon-copper may be coming to an end. Very shortly I expect Chisholm and Jones to be touching their caps as we drive past. So I'd better give Charley Hooper a bell.'

'Who's Charley Hooper?'

'Stage manager down the Hearts of Oak. He owes me at least three. He worked off one of them by getting me the contract for supplying the chairs. That leaves two more. So there shouldn't be no trouble getting him to introduce me to the producer or director or whatever. And when we get to the first night, Tel, I'll expect you to be in the front row. Surrounded by as many birds as you can persuade to come. And all of you clapping like hell.'

Two days later I presented myself by appointment at the Hearts of Oak at half past two in the afternoon. Charley Hooper had fixed for me to meet Ambrose Kelly, the director of the play, although he had warned:

'He don't mind seeing you, Arfur. But he told me 'e don't need no new actors at present. Got all 'e needs for 'is present production of *Julius Caesar*.'

Naturally I had been a bit put down by this news but I figured that if I gave a good audition I'd be in with a chance for the next production. So I went ahead with the meet.

I had dressed very carefully for the occasion and was wearing a suit of pink velvet that a tailor friend of mine had run up from some slightly warehouse-soiled material I'd failed to shift after years of trying, a big green silk cravat and a broad-brimmed black hat. I'd also purchased some pink cigarettes and a long cigarette-holder to strengthen

*I must have a
poet's nature*

the costume for I had figured out that to stand any
chance I would have to begin by acting the part of
an actor. So I'd copied my costume from a picture
of Ivor Novello that I'd found in a book about the
theatre which I'd got from the library.

Terry grinned when he saw me in it. And
Ambrose Kelly seemed a little surprised too. But
after a faint raising of the eyebrows he greeted me
in a very friendly way.

'I hear you'd like to join us, Arthur?'

We was seated at the back of the little theatre
while people was messing about with sets and
lights on the stage. Ambrose was a graceful man of
about forty, wearing jeans and a T-shirt, that I'd
discovered was the art master at the local
comprehensive. Knowing some of the thuggish
youngsters who infested the streets round the
school I wondered how he managed to keep
discipline in his job.

'Would I not?' I replied. 'It's in my blood,
you see: the smell of greasepaint, the thunder of
applause.'

'I see. Well – TOO HIGH, CHARLEY!
TAKE IT DOWN AT LEAST A FOOT!'

So now I knew how he kept discipline in class.
He had a voice like a bullhorn when he cared
to wield it. I shook my head slightly to try and
suppress the faint ringing his bellow at his stage
manager had induced. He resumed in the pleasant,
mild voice with which he'd greeted me:

'Might I enquire what you do, Arthur?'

'Certainly. I'm a member – probably be fair to
say, a prominent member – of the Fulham business
community. I'm surprised you never heard of me,
as a matter of fact.'

'Actually I think Bats may have mentioned you.
That's Bats Basildon who's head of the local CID.
He's a wonderful raconteur. He delights us quite

often with his imitations of local villains. Yes, but that could hardly include you, could it?'

'Hardly.'

'You've got a very interesting face. Do you always wear that pink suit?'

'Well, not for my commercial life, no. But it somehow expresses my inner, artistic nature.'

'And it doesn't bother you? I mean, the inevitable tug-of-war between the two sides of your nature? Have you done any acting before?'

'Not since school. Nothing makes me sadder. Because it leaves a big hole in my cultural life. But I think now I can find the time to get back to it.'

'I'd have to give you an audition.'

'Of course.'

'And then – FOR GOD'S SAKE, CHARLEY, FLY IT, DON'T ROLL IT!'

He turned back to me.

'Well, the current situation is, Mr Daley –'

'Oh, I know you're fully cast for *Julius Caesar*. I'm chiefly thinking of your next production or the one after that.'

'You like Shakespeare, do you?'

'Like him? Most evenings I curl up in bed with one of his great masterpieces – for at least an hour before turning out the light. 'Er indoors is always saying: "Can't understand what you see in all that old 'gadzooks' stuff, Arthur. It's not even lifelike." But I reckon I must have a poet's nature. Shakespeare never fails to bring tears to my eyes.'

'I see. How do you feel about Ligarius?'

'Well, I wouldn't put him in the same league as Shakespeare but I reckon he's still a very interesting playwriter what –'

'I was really thinking of the character Ligarius in *Julius Caesar*. YES, RIGHT THERE, CHARLEY! Oh, sorry did I startle you? A director is a bit like a sergeant major. You were saying, Arthur?'

'I was just saying about the character Lig– er Lig–'

'Ligarius.'

'Yeah, him. I reckon he's a very interesting character but not got as much depth as one of the all-time greats like Hamlet.'

'No, well that may be because Ligarius only has five short speeches altogether. But the point is we've lost our Ligarius. He's an airline pilot and he's been sent on a course to learn to fly bigger and better aeroplanes. Would you like to have a stab at Ligarius?'

'A stab at him? You mean with a dagger?'

'Well – he'll certainly carry a dagger. As a prop.'

'So we'll both have daggers?'

'Er – both of whom?'

'Both Ligarius and me.'

'I think we've got our wires crossed somewhere. What I'm trying to say is that Ligarius, who is one of the conspirators – I say, you do know *Julius Caesar*, don't you?'

'Oh, intimately. Terrific stuff.'

'Well, many productions cut Ligarius –'

'What, with the dagger?'

'I think perhaps we should try to forget the dagger. What I'm saying is that many directors cut the character out of their productions altogether. But in my opinion the short scene between Brutus and Ligarius is a microcosm of the whole play. It encapsulates the very essence of *Julius Caesar*. You recall, of course, Brutus's speech: "A piece of work that will make sick men whole"?'

'I do. Sheer magic.'

'Then you presumably also remember what Ligarius replies?'

'Perhaps you could just refresh my memory?'

'He turns the words triumphantly inside out: "But are not some whole that we must make sick?" Isn't that marvellous?'

'Unbelievable.'

'Well why don't I get a couple of scripts and we can read through the scene together?'

'Can't wait to get my teeth into it.'

In fact, we went through it three times together. And I have to confess that Ambrose did not respond with what I would regard as wild enthusiasm towards my rendition of Ligarius. The fact is that my performance definitely was a bit shaky because I couldn't really make head or tail of what Ligarius was getting at. When we'd finished doing it for the third time, Ambrose was silent for a while, nodding from time to time. Then he seemed to pull himself together and flashed me a quick smile.

'Yes, well, there are one or two other chaps coming in to audition. At least I'm pretty sure there are – with any luck. But I'll let you know, Arthur.'

'Fine. And if I don't get the part, I'd be happy to help out any other way I could, looking after the bar perhaps or something more menial still. I just want to immerse myself in the wonderful world of showbiz.'

But – and this was a turn-up – I did get the part. Ambrose phoned the next day with the good news, although he didn't sound specially joyous. It was some time later I learned that he hadn't had any other takers for it and had spent much of the previous day trying to persuade someone to do it. He had only accepted me in desperation. I can say all this without feeling any sense of failure because, as you already know, my only reason for joining the troupe was to try and pal up with 'Batty' Basildon. And in this I was completely successful

'Batty' making up and me making up to Batty

all through the rehearsal period. I think the secret of my success with Batty was that I brought to bear on the challenge the deep instinct for what makes a bloke tick that I used in all my commercial dealings. After sizing up Batty for several sessions of rehearsal before I approached him, I came to the conclusion that what made Batty tick, as an actor at least, was vanity. So I approached him with an autograph book and pen held out. And from that moment on we were as thick as – well, chief superintendents.

'Was I all right, Arthur?' he would turn to me and ask after a run-through of one of his big scenes.

'You was terrific,' I would assure him, dabbing at the corner of my eye with a kleenex. 'When you said that line about night hanging down from your tongue –'

'Eyes.'

'That's right "eyes". How does it go?'

At which Batty would stand up in his short skirt and touch his broadsword and declaim:

Lord John Olivier

'Night hangs upon mine eyes; my bones would rest that have but labour'd to attain this hour.'

'Wonderful, wonderful. Sir Laurence Gielgud couldn't have done no better.'

By this time, I had become Batty's inseparable companion. He came to me for help, advice and applause and I could see that Ambrose was sometimes a little put out by how close we had become. Mind you I never saw Batty outside the theatre but in it we was like brothers. We had meals together in the canteen, drinks in the bar and very often he applied to me to hear him say his lines or for advice about costumes or make-up. But, as I said, thus far our friendship was purely theatrical and that was just how I wanted it. I had no intention of confusing matters yet by complaining to him about harassment from Chisholm and Jones. There would be time for that later when *Julius Caesar* was the success of the Fulham theatrical year and Batty was in my debt for ever. After that, woe betide Chisholm if he even so much as slapped a parking ticket on my windscreen. I'd get Batty to bounce him out of the local CID quicker than Brutus had put the knife into Caesar.

There was only one thing which slightly clouded relations between Batty Basildon and me. And that was his having to be on at me the whole time to learn my part. I hadn't done so properly because the period of rehearsals happened to coincide with a very busy time for me when I had a lock-up full of very high quality but low-priced jewellery from Thailand and retailers from all over South London scooping it up by the vanload. Also I must confess that, despite my lifelong devotion to the Bard's immortal lines, learning poetry by heart has never been my strong point. It took me most of my school years to master the first verse of 'God Save the Queen'. Naturally whenever I could snatch a moment I got out my script and slogged away at my part but when it came time to rehearse it with the chief super most of it had slipped from my mind again. Even at the dress rehearsal I still had to use the script to read from. The occasion was a great success as could be judged by the applause from the invited audience. But after it was over, Batty said to me in his dressing room:

'Arthur, you won't let me down tomorrow, will you? I mean if you made me look a fool on stage it's not something I would find easy to forgive.'

'Now, Bats, would I do a thing like that? The fact is that after leaving the theatre this evening I am going straight home and I am going to work non-stop on my lines for the next twenty-four hours, pausing only to catch a nap or two. By tomorrow night I'll know the scene forwards, backwards and upside down. So put aside all anxiety, Bats. It will go like clockwork on the night.'

And I believed every word I spoke. After all, as Ambrose had informed me the first time we'd ever met, the scene only had five short speeches by Ligarius in it. So even taking into account my resistance to cluttering up my brain with poetry, I could hardly fail to get that much by heart in the time available.

But, of course, the time turned out not to be all that available after all. First off 'er indoors went to sleep in the bath with the tap running and the bath overflowed and water poured down the stairs. What with trying to get a flying plumber to pay a call for a fee that would be less than the national debt and in the meanwhile striving to keep the happy home from turning into something resembling a peat-bog, the evening before opening night passed without me so much as glancing at my script.

The next day, my car wouldn't start and frantic

phone calls to the AA, interspersed with sessions of opening the bonnet and gazing reproachfully at the engine, took up most of the morning. And in the afternoon, I had no option but to meet three Japanese who were only in London for the one day and had a line in near-silk kimonos which simply couldn't be ignored. The upshot was that I only got down to serious studying over my tea. None the less when I set off for the theatre, a couple of hours later, with 'er indoors wearing her best party dress in honour of the occasion and looking quite delightful seated next to me in the remobilised Jag, I felt absolutely confident that I wouldn't let Batty down.

So what I totally fail to comprehend is how it can all completely disappear like that! At half past seven I knew my lines perfectly. At half past eight when, clad in my white sheet and girded with my dagger, I stood on stage opposite Batty while he, sounding somewhat like a Red Indian chief, greeted me, 'Caius Ligarius. How? I couldn't remember one single word!

I tried for some seconds to draw up from the depths of my mind something – anything – that Shakespeare might have written in reply to Batty's Cherokee greeting. Meanwhile, as I could hardly fail to observe since our noses was almost touching, a look of concern had begun to form on the Chief Super's face.

Finally, and although I knew very well that it was not the right line, I managed to eject: 'How, Brutus!'

And after this tribal exchange how I wished the two of us could, instead of talking any more, simply go into a war dance with much whooping and leaping. But unhappily Batty stuck to the script.

'O what a time have you chose out, brave Caius, to wear a kerchief! Would you were not sick!'

Kerchief? Sick? Was I wearing a kerchief? Oh right, the dresser had rushed over and tied one round my neck just before I went on stage. But what was my line? What kind of sickness required the wearing of a kerchief? Then I detected a faint muttering and my heart leaped. It was the prompter. But the imbecile wasn't talking loud enough. I couldn't quite catch the words. Meanwhile a throaty stirring was sounding from the audience and Batty was glaring at me. Sick? I opened my mouth and improvised:

"Tis only a slight touch of flu, Brutus. The kerchief's just in case I need to blow my nose. So you can talk quite freely. I'm not delirious or nothing.'

With an incredulous, but relatively soft, exclamation, Batty proclaimed:

'Such an exploit have I in hand, Ligarius. Had you a healthful ear to hear of it.'

Exploit? What exploit? Idiot, I reproached myself. What's the bloody play about? Killing Caesar, isn't it? So that must be the exploit Batty's on about. Yes, but what's my line? Desperately, I improvised again.

'Hasn't affected my ears or nothing. Tell me what you're plotting, Brutus. I'd really like to know.'

Batty gasped as if in sudden pain but rallied and went on:

'A piece of work that will make sick men whole.'

Of course, this was the bit that Ambrose thought was so brilliant. But did it help knowing that? Not a whole lot. I took a deep breath and plunged on:

'Even so, there are quite a few whole men that make you sick, wouldn't you agree, Batty? Er, Brutus?'

Batty snapped, and, not even trying to keep his voice down, snarled:

'You idiot!'

'I'm really sorry,' I apologised, keeping it low. 'I just forgot a few lines.'

'You're ruining the whole thing.'

I was again aware of a background murmur and this time there was no mistaking what it was. It was laughter. The whole audience seemed to be in stitches. I whispered:

'I'll try harder. We better get on with it.'

I have to hand it to Batty. He had guts. It was the same guts which had enabled him, on an occasion famous in the annals of the Metropolitan Police, to tackle a whole firm of tea-leaves that was carrying shooters all on his own when his back-up had failed to show. Now once again his back-up had let him down but he soldiered on:

Also known as 'The Arthur Daley of Greece'

'That must we also. What is it, my Caius, I shall unfold to thee, as we are going to whom it must be done.'

Please, please! I implored the Gods of drama. Give me the bloody line!

But it was no use. It was time for Daley's last stand.

'It must be done to Caesar, am I not right, brave Brutus? We must surround him in the Capitol and put the boot in. Well, the dagger in. So lead on, Noble Brutus. To the Capitol. How.'

'Damn you!' screamed Batty and seized me by the throat.

In a moment we was rolling around on the stage and a moment after that the curtain was lowered. And of the remainder of that painful evening no more need be said.

The next morning.

'Here comes bad news,' muttered Tel thickly, his mouth full of bacon sandwich.

I glanced out of the window. A small unmarked car had pulled up and two men were getting out.

'It is the bright day that brings forth the adder,' I said gloomily.

'Eh?'

'Line from Shakespeare. *Julius Caesar*, as it happens.'

Chisholm and Jones entered the caff and approached our table. Chisholm smiled and I was mildly interested to note that his eyes took part in the genial display. It was the first time I had ever seen this happen.

'Good morning, Arthur,' he said warmly. 'Mind if we join you? Don't seem to be any other empty places.'

I glanced about glumly. But it was true. The Mighty Munch Café was packed with its usual breakfast crowd, mostly building labourers.

'I suppose you've come to gloat?' I said with a sigh.

'Gloat?' repeated Chisholm in pretend astonishment. 'What about? We've come to congratulate, haven't we, Jones?'

He pointed to the *South London Gazette* lying on the table beside my mug of tea and went on:

'As you've seen yourself, Arthur, almost the whole review of last night's performance is devoted to your very small part in the play. You've achieved overnight fame.'

'Very funny,' I muttered.

'So the reviewer insists. One of the funniest things he's ever seen on a stage apparently. He also said that when you and the Chief Super rolled off the edge of it locked in each other's arms and straight into the laps of the front row audience he feared that he might choke to death from laughing. You've certainly written a new chapter in Fulham theatrical history, Arthur.'

'Yeah, well –' was about the strongest retort I could summon.

'What puzzles me,' continued Chisholm, 'is why you took the part in the first place. Now Jones here is an authority on all matters artistic and, like me, he was in the auditorium last night. How would you describe Mr Daley's performance, Jones?'

'No good. He has no talent for acting.'

'That's what I would have said. And the Hearts of Oak don't pay their performers so it can't be simple greed. Could the fact that Chief Superintendent Basildon, who is a very well-known amateur actor, was taking the lead have had anything to do with the decision? Was that it, Arthur?'

'Certainly not. I've always had a yen to try my hand as a performer, haven't I, Tel?'

Terry gazed at me in astonishment for a moment but rallied.

'What? Oh yeah, Arthur sees himself as a sort of cross between Humphrey Bogart and Lassie.'

Chisholm nodded affably.

'Well, I'm glad it had nothing to do with ingratiating yourself with the Chief Super, Arthur. Because if that had been the motive one would have to report that it has proved a spectacular failure. As Mr Basildon perused that review this morning, I could actually hear him rumbling with fury like Krakatoa about to blow its top. I should think you're less *persona grata* with him than any villain – or should I say any other villain? – in Fulham just at present. Still, you have to admit that old Basildon is a trouper. When the unparalleled scenes of riot and hilarity had died down he actually went on with his performance. And what's more he did very well. I would even go so far as to maintain that he approached true greatness in that superb speech: "There is a tide in the affairs of men which, taken at the flood, leads

on to fortune: omitted, all the voyage of their life is bound in shallows and in miseries."'

Chisholm glanced towards the counter where the staff of three was besieged by customers.

'No good, Jones. Take us too long to get served. So, Arthur, we'll take our leave of you for the present. But I can promise you that from now on you'll see even more of us than you have done in the past. Can you guess why?'

My instinct was to tell the charmless sleuth to get stuffed. But curiosity got the better of me.

'Why?'

'That tide, Arthur – the one in the affairs of men. You missed it good and proper. So from now on your life is going to be bound in shallows and in miseries. That means me and Jones. Isn't that right, Jones? Jones, don't forget there are felons out there waiting to be apprehended. So I do hope you're not going to lapse into one of your trances. Goodbye, Arthur. See you on the Ides of March – if not before.'

And with one of his old-style smiles that started beneath the eyes, and a nudge in the ribs to his inert subordinate, Chisholm turned and stalked out of the caff.

'Arthur sees himself,' said Tel, 'as a cross between Humphrey Bogart and Lassie'

CHAPTER EIGHT
THE CHISHOLM YEARS

A ND TO SHOW THAT, in spite of the terrible time I had with the Bard, I bear no grudge against him, I will begin this chapter with a little quotation from his immortal works: 'Be some bloke as white as snow some rotten cop will besmirch his reputation.'

I believe that comes from *Hamlet* but it may be from one of his other plays with tragic heroes. Well, all I can say is Hamlet, Othello, Macfudge and the other tragic heroes of Shakespeare were in clover compared to what I was in during the long, painful years when I had Chisholm breathing down my neck day and night. I could not park the Jag in the street without Chisholm leaping out of a shop doorway to affix a ticket to its windscreen. If I met a fellow businessman for a discreet conference which, to thwart industrial espionage, we had arranged to conduct in the public loo down Vine Street, we had only to reach down for our zips for a cabinet door to snap open and Chisholm to spring out with a notebook or microrecorder at the ready.

One could not get into conversation with a friendly stranger in some boozer without noticing, at some point in the chat, a few little bits of flex under the other's string vest and realising that, somewhere nearby, Chisholm was parked on his butt in an unmarked van listening in to what one had thus far assumed was merely an idle chat with a pleasant new acquaintance but what was really a skilled grilling by a plain-clothes copper.

And what was it all about? Who is to judge

£ Because of the malignant attentions of this rabid rozzer, England has been deprived of someone who could have gone down in the history books amongst such great names as John Major, Winston Churchill and Pitt the Youngster

the human heart? The Bard had something to say about that too, if I remember rightly. Was it not in *Romeo and Juliet* that one of the minor characters proclaims: 'Though black villainy may stand a round now and then what price a heart of gold?' Not sure I've got that exactly right. But the point of it is that there is no way you can tell just by looking at a chap whether he's straight or bent. In the old days, there was a thing called physiognomy which meant judging people by how they looked. Criminals was supposed to have close-set eyes and narrow lips and honest men had full lips, big round eyes and so on. But it's all hooey. Science has proved that it is impossible to tell anything about a bloke's character just from clocking his jem mace. If you show a man in the street pictures of grade A villains and of saints all mixed up, he (the man in the street) will not be able to tell any difference between them. He might say, 'This rat-faced fellow here is clearly a terrible crook.' But in fact it's just as likely to be Saint Aloysius of Boloney or someone equally noble. So what I am getting at is: what can have induced Chisholm to target me for his hound-like attentions in the first place?

The thing is, Chisholm himself looks very like a cross between a rat and a ferret and what's more, in spite of science, really does have a nature very similar to both of the two unpleasant animals I have named. But we must assume that Chisholm does not start back in horror whenever he has a shave with a cry of: that fellow staring at me is a villain if ever I saw one! So then, whatever his attitude to my appearance, where the hell did he first get the notion that I was bent? This is especially puzzling in that I am, as everyone who knows me well will testify, almost painfully honest in all my commercial and human transactions.

Now that it is all over and I have won I can be

Great names like John Major, Winston Churchill and Arthur Daley

magnanimous about the deranged detective. But it would be trifling with the truth not to state very loud and clear that Chisholm has done a great deal of harm to human society. For the fact is that Chisholm came snarling into my life like a mad dog just as my career was about to peak. I had become a thriving and respected businessman whose enterprise, keen intelligence and schemes for social improvement was just beginning to catch the attention of them at the top. I had received intimations on several occasions that before very long I might be invited to stand for the council and soon after that for Parliament. From then on, I would doubtless rapidly have assumed my rightful place in the establishment and might even one day have carried on my Jaguar keyring the latchkey to a particular little terraced house in Downing Street.

But it was not to be and my loss is nothing compared to the nation's. Because of the malignant attentions of this rabid rozzer, England has been deprived of someone who could have gone down in the history books amongst such great names as John Major, Winston Churchill and Pitt the Youngster. So the present chapter is really the story of just one round in the age old punch-up between good and evil. Chisholm is, of course, the evil one and I the good.

It began when Gus Samson went bust owing me a very substantial sum for goods supplied. Since the nature of the transactions between us had been designed to reduce the tax burden for both Gus and me, it would have been difficult to obtain redress for my losses in court. Terry and I therefore went round for a chat with Gus to see if we could reach an agreement and come to some amicable settlement. But it soon became apparent that, despite all the eloquence that either Terry or

I acquired leases on two Indian restaurants

I could muster, Gus was simply not in a position to stump up any more lolly. The only thing of value that he could offer was the short-term leases on two Indian restaurants that had been part of his, to put it mildly, very rickety commercial empire.

I knew these establishments chiefly from having on several occasions declined invitations to dine in them. I'd been put off by their dismal appearance and even more so by their reputations for serving disgusting food. You will guess, therefore, that it was not with any very great enthusiasm that I accepted Gus's offer. However, I felt that both caffs could be converted into sandwich bars or something similar so that they would at least earn their keep. However, something that happened soon after I became their owner caused me to think again. I chanced to nosh one lunchtime with a party of discriminating foodies at a small but stylish Indian restaurant on the borders between Fulham and Chelsea. Three of us ordered Lamb vindaloo and we were all three staggered by the richness and power of the dish. We enthused to each other about its excellence even as we gasped for breath, wiped our streaming eyes and repeatedly gulped great draughts of healing mineral water. Indeed Monty Podsnap was so deeply affected by the meal that he felt it necessary to take off and reel round the block, gasping and choking, before returning to resume his feast.

Now one of the diners was a bloke who went under the name of Major Erskine. He was supposed to have spent a lot of time in India. I had heard rumours that he had never, in spite of his name, served in any branch of Her Majesty's forces but had made a career out of giving investment advice to wealthy Indians. Apparently some misunderstanding had arisen over a parcel of bees and honey he had offered to invest for one of them but had then forgotten about because his aunty had died. He had, as a result, found himself at odds with the Indian police. So he had returned to England by a scenic route through the Himalayas. But the point is that this Major Erskine proclaimed that the vindaloo we had just consumed was the best he had ever tasted except for one he had eaten in a small caff in Bombay run by a bloke called Rahman Singh. Ever attentive for ways to improve my own commercial enterprises, I summoned the head waiter, congratulated him in a hoarse voice on his curry and asked him what curry powder he had used. Imagine my astonishment when he replied:

'Oh that, Sahib, that is Rahman Singh's Herbal

Gunpowder.'

'Good Lord,' exclaimed Major Erskine.

Naturally there was a good deal of laughter and chaff at this strange coincidence. I then asked the head waiter:

'Where could I get a supply of Rahman Singh's curry?'

He answered:

'There is only one supplier for the whole of England and that is Ahmed Patel, whom everyone calls Big Ahmed. You see – it is a little hard to explain – but this curry powder is so strong, so rich, so – so good that it is forbidden.'

'How do you mean forbidden?' I naturally asked in astonishment.

'It is on the banned list. It is a prohibited import. It contains some spice or herbs – I don't know what they are – but they make some people shiver with delight. So you can only get it from Big Ahmed.'

The Source of Rahman's Singh's Herbal gunpowder

'And where,' I asked, trying to suppress an impulse to giggle with joy, 'can I contact this Big Ahmed?'

'If you wait one moment, Sahib,' promised the head waiter courteously. 'I will get you his address.'

And he did just that. I was not surprised to find out that it was in that little corner of Fulham centered on Dungannon Street where a lot of Pakistanis and Indians live. I have always had a deep respect for my fellow businessmen from the sub-continent since I find them to be, on the whole, a hard-working, if also hard-bargaining, and totally honest group of people. And if they choose to take their holidays seated at their cash registers well some people just don't feel the need for a change, do they?

Nevertheless, on the morning I set out in my Jaguar saloon to negotiate with the fellow known familiarly as Big Ahmed I was not entirely at ease. But I was not sure what was the cause of my discomfort. I had not, as far as I could remember, ever encountered Big Ahmed in my numerous contacts with the local trading community and yet whenever I tested the name on my tongue I felt a small shock of alarm. What could it mean? By the time I pulled up outside a tall narrow, terraced house – the address I had been given – I had decided that some rumour or item of gossip concerning Big Ahmed must have come my way and that, because it had not been too comforting, I would do well to be cautious.

But my slight nervousness was much calmed soon after I had rung the doorbell. For the door was opened, after a short delay, by one of the most beautiful creatures I have ever seen in my life. She was perhaps in her mid-twenties, had straight, raven-black hair and a little red marriage

dot on her brow. She was wearing an emerald green
sari which, with its bare midriff, did little to prevent
the appreciative viewer from speculating as to what
other perfections might still be concealed. She had
a light-brown complexion and two dark brown eyes
and her lips formed a most perfect bow. I was in
fact quite bowled over.

'Hello,' I exclaimed, touching my hat in respect
and offering a heartfelt smile. 'Do I have the pleasure of addressing Mrs Ahmed Patel?'

'Oh yes.'

'Then I wonder if I could ask you where I might
find your esteemed husband?'

'Oh no. Not here. Big Ahmed is – he is
not here.'

But I could not help noticing that, even as she
said it, she glanced over her shoulder nervously.
Perhaps, I thought to myself, the distributor of the
magical herbal gunpowder is being cagey. Perhaps
he is cautious about customers since his curry is,
for some reason, on the banned list.

'It's all right,' I said soothingly. 'I'm in business
like your husband. I'm opening a couple of new
curry houses in Fulham and I hoped to acquire
some of your husband's wonderful Herbal Gunpowder for my chef. But if Big Ah – that is your
honoured husband – is out, perhaps I could make
an appointment to see him at his convenience? I
only want a very small amount of his product in
the first place, just to see if my chef can handle
such a – well such a dynamic product.'

She nodded rapidly.

'All right. You come with me. You want sample? I give you sample. You come with me.'

She turned and teetered prettily to a door a
little way down the corridor. She opened it and led
the way inside. It was a smallish chamber without
a window and with a plain cement floor and bare

walls. All round the room were white fabric sacks stained a vivid yellow by the escape of curry powder. This substance had also accumulated on all ledges and in patches on the floor while the air itself was mistily yellow with floating curry. At the first breath I exploded into a paroxysm of sneezing and coughing but, even as I rocked and rolled about the room I could feel happy sensations stealing over me. Mrs Patel, clearly not unaccustomed to this kind of reaction from customers, waited patiently. Then when I had recovered something of my usual courtliness and poise, she led me over to a sack that was clearly only partly full, pulled aside the flaps of cloth and, with a little scoop, dipped me out a few ounces of curry powder. She put this in a little plastic bag which she took from a pile on a low shelf and handed it towards me. But just as my hand went out to receive it I was frozen by a kind of outraged gasp from behind me. Then, in a voice like a striking snake's, a voice hissed:

'You! The thief!'

Naturally I turned at once. And the first thing that was made clear to me was why I had not known from his name who Ahmed Patel really was. It is true that I had only had any dealings with him on one former occasion and that had been some three or four years before. Moreover it had been Terry who had chiefly handled the transaction. None the less I would have immediately recalled my meeting with Mr Patel but for one thing. The last time we had met I had not known his nickname, Big Ahmed. So naturally enough when the head waiter had mentioned someone called 'Big' Ahmed, I had concluded that the person referred to must be tall and/or bulky. But now I perceived that Ahmed was known as 'Big' the way Little John in the story of Robin Hood was known as 'Little'. That is, it was a joke. For the person who now stood glaring at me from the door and menacing me with a fist about the size of a Brussels sprout was a tiny bloke not much above five feet tall and not much fatter than a credit card. For all that, I shuddered and retreated a step or two. The last time I had seen Ahmed Patel, which was as he had pursued me round my car yard waving a curved dagger which I afterwards learned he had inherited from a warrior father, I had perceived very clearly that he was not someone to be trifled with.

I quickly glanced about for an escape route but there was no conceivable way out of the small chamber but by way of the door where 'Big' Ahmed was now stationed. I weighed in my mind the relative merits of seizing Mrs Patel and holding her before me like a shield or of scooping up a handful of herbal gunpowder and trying to blind the dwarf with it. But neither scheme seemed very promising and so, since Mr Patel did not seem, on this occasion, to be armed with his curved dagger or any other weapons, I decided to attempt diplomacy.

'Mr Patel, is it?' I asked, smiling warmly. 'Do you know I have an idea that we may have met before somewhere?'

'Oh yes. We met. When you sold me the car with the square wheels.'

I winced but tried to conceal it. It seemed that the memory of his grievance was as fresh as his curry powder.

'Square wheels?' I repeated, with an incredulous smile. 'They don't make cars like that.'

'No. But you get one. And you keep it for a sucker. And you think I am the sucker. And so you sell it to me.'

'Ah, I think I'm zeroing in now. You're saying that you were dissatisfied with a vehicle we supplied you, is that it?'

£ I realised at long last that Chisholm was in the grip of an irresistible compulsion to deprive me of my freedom

'Yes. I was not satisfied. Who would be satisfied with car with square wheels?'

'Mr Patel, if the vehicle – a nice little runner as I recall – had really had square wheels you would have spotted it right off and you wouldn't have bought it.'

'Wheels not very square. Not to see square. To feel square. When you drive, car go thumbo, thumbo thumbo.'

It seemed to me there was little point in trying to explain to Mr Patel that the thumping which had distressed him had probably been caused by a defective gear train which some scoundrel had probably tried to conceal by putting sawdust in the gear box. No, it was best to try and put the past behind us.

'Well, it was a long time ago, Mr Patel. But I was just telling your wife how much I appreciate your superb herbal gunpowder –'

'No curry for thieves.'

'But I assure you, Mr Patel, I have in mind only a perfectly normal commercial transaction. Your dear wife has just generously provided me with this sample but in the near future I hope to place a substantial order for Rahman Singh's dynamite for my two new Indian restaurants and –'

'Drop the curry!'

This time I winced openly and shut my eyes for an instant. The curved dagger, which was about as long as the little chap's arm, had appeared mysteriously from the depths of his clothing.

'As you say, Mr Patel –' I murmured soothingly and held up my arms to show that I myself was without a weapon. 'Well then, it's been a pleasant little reunion but all good things must come to an end. So I'll just jog along without the gunpowder, it seems. All right then – I'll quietly depart. And I do hope that pigsticker isn't sharpened and that you realise, Mr Patel, that there are severe penalties in this country for those who carve up their fellow men. So – no hard feelings on my part and I trust I'm right in assuming that you feel the same. So – as I said –'

And keeping up this somewhat desperate line of patter, more to distract than to convince the little demon, I slowly approached the door where he stood guard and then very gently edged around him, gasping once as the dagger seemed to twitch in his grasp, and so finally out into the passage, down to the front door and then through it to the street. Having reached this public haven I made a dash for my car, slid into the driving seat, started the engine and, a quivering wreck but still miraculously unpunctured, took off with an ear-splitting roar.

Right, thought I, when my nerves had stopped leaping like salmon at a waterfall, there's more than one way to skin a cat and there must be any number of ways of acquiring a few dollops of Rahman Singh's Herbal Gunpowder.

But I was wrong.

The obvious way, of course, was to negotiate the purchase of the amount I required from some other restaurateur who was in the Demon Dwarf's good books and could buy it for me. But it turned out there was no such benefactor. Rahman Singh's treasure proved to be gold dust indeed. So little of it was imported by Big Ahmed that no recipient that I could find would part with a single ounce. Indeed they all grumbled that they could not get enough for their own use and that the stuff was more valuable, in fact, than the same weight of gold dust would have been. Once tasted, for ever addicted, seemed to describe diners who came under its spell. My next attempt consisted of trying to get the stuff analysed so that I could make some of my own. But it proved to be such a complicated concoction containing so many rare plants that it defeated the hi-tech laboratory run by a friend of mine who made French-style perfumes.

So at that point I pretty well gave up and ordered in the decorators to convert my two Indian caffs into sandwich bars. But before work could start, I happened to be describing the whole tabasco to Dave one evening, as an example of the numerous obstacles that come between an entrepreneur and his profits, and when I reached the part about the beautiful wife opening the door, Dave asked:

'Which one?'

'Which one what?'

'Which wife?'

'Patel's wife, like I said.'

'But which one. He's got four.'

'Don't be ridiculous. That's illegal – not to mention masochistic.'

'It may be illegal here but it's what they all gets up to in – in them countries.'

'What countries?'

'Where the blokes is called musclemen or muslins or something like that. Four wives is their standard ration. 'Course when they get over here a lot of them make do with one but they is entitled to four each.'

I gazed at Dave, upon receiving this information, with what could be called a wild surmise. For I had perceived a way to obtain the precious gunpowder.

No, not blackmail. Not extortion. Which is ugly words. Just what I would call the creative use of industrial espionage. What I had in mind was getting the little firebrand on the dog and suggesting a mutually beneficial arrangement. He would supply me with all the Herbal Gunpowder I required and I would do my utmost to ensure that knowledge of what might be called his overprivileged status in the marriage stakes never reached the ears of the dreaded Home Office Marriage Inspectors. What? You has never heard of this splendid body of men? Well, all I can say is that the mere mention of them was enough to produce a long silence at the other end of the wire. And then a deal was quite quickly struck. The very next day one of Patel's other three wives, who looked, a little surprisingly after the vision I had already encountered, somewhat like a Russian lorry driver, turned up at the lock-up with a two-kilo sack of the duodenum-busting gold powder.

It was a day or two later, when Terry and I were going over the premises of one of our Indian caffs to be, planning its décor and discussing staffing problems, that a voice containing an evil sneer said:

'Have you considered a stylish arrangement of barred windows and bare stttttone walls?'

Without glancing in the direction of the voice, I said to Terry:

'You must have forgot to close the front door, Terence. I'm sure I heard the yapping of a stray dog which must have wandered in.'

It was a bit naughty and for a moment I thought it might provoke an explosion of fury but the voice resumed, pleasantly enough:

'Nice try, Daley. But we're feeling far too happy today to take offence at your clumsy insults, aren't we, Jones?'

'Hm?' enquired the Welsh rozzer vaguely. 'Oh yes, that's the truth, Sarge.'

'Do strive to stay awake, Jones,' urged Chisholm in a weary voice. 'At least when we're actually about to nab a big-time villain.'

I must have started a bit at this for, with a nasty intonation, Chisholm continued:

*'Bang to rights,
this time, Daley!'*

'That's right, Daley. The time has come for heavy keys groaning in massive steel gates. Bang to rights, this time.'

Hoping I looked, as I felt, completely non-plussed, I smiled and asked:

'Would it be in order for me to enquire what felony you are implying I have committed, Mr Chisholm?'

'Perfectly in order, Daley. How does drug-dealing grab you?'

'I think you must be confusing me with that Columbian geezer. I don't own any cocaine forests, Mr Chisholm.'

He chuckled evilly.

'Oh, not big-time drug-dealing, Daley. No connection with night drops from light aircraft. Not a case of vast profits stacked in Swiss bank accounts. But drug-dealing none the less. I believe you have in your possession a bag of golden substance known as Rahman Singh's Herbal Gunpowder. Is that correct?'

'Quite correct, Mr Chisholm. I am basing the fortunes of my two new Fulham eateries, which will, I trust, soon be the place of choice to dine for the top people of our happy parish, on that wonderful spice.'

'Wonderful but illicit, Daley.'

'How do you mean?'

'It induces euphoria. Haven't you noticed?'

'What exactly is me-phoria, Mr Chisholm?'

'I always had you down as a bit of a scholar, Daley. The word "euphoria", from the Greek, means delight, excessive happiness, even unnatural mirth and merriment – a state quite often generated by the use of narcotics.'

'Like curry powder?'

'Like this particular curry powder. Rahman Singh's herbal gunpowder includes, amongst its more innocuous ingredients, opium, indian hemp, a suspicion of cocaine and a sprinkling of mixed hallucinogens. It is, in fact, a kind of pusher's dream drug, the mind-blowing cocktail that eluded even the hippies. Which is why international drug enforcement agents have been trying to track it, and its suppliers, down for some time.'

A twinge of genuine alarm now gripped me.

'But hang about, Mr Chisholm, even if all this is true –'

'Oh, it most certainly is true, Daley.'

'Yeah but I didn't know, did I? You can't charge a bloke with being a drug baron just because he innocently buys a packet of curry powder.'

Chisholm smiled like a German general contemplating a map of Poland.

'I can try.'

'I shall plead victimisation. I don't think you'll

get very far. You'll never convince a fair-minded
English court that Arthur Daley is a drug dealer.'

Chisholm shook his head in mock dismay.

'Oh dear. Well, in that case how about black-
mailer?'

I shook my head in total bafflement.

'You've lost me again, Mr Chisholm.'

'Actually I was beginning to fear that I *had*
lost you, Arthur. And then, to my delight, two
agents of the American Drug Enforcement Agency
came up with something very handy. No? Still not
plugged in to my line of thought? The fact is they
had Patel's telephone tapped, Daley. And they
heard you blackmailing him to supply you with
the drug. You see the beauty of the thing from my
point of view? We get you coming and going. You
would hardly have stooped to something as bent
as blackmail just to obtain curry powder, would
you? So each felony reinforces the other. Yes, I
have high hopes that you'll be off the streets, and
so out of my hair, for an appreciable spell, Arthur
Daley.'

It took something of an effort of will but I managed a weak laugh meant to convey scepticism.

'There wasn't any blackmail. I suppose you're
referring to the little joke I played on Patel?'

'That's right, Arthur, the little joke. And you'd
better pray the jury shares your sense of humour.
They'll probably roll about in the aisles of the court
when we play them the tape of your threatening
Patel with exposure of his multiple bigamy unless
he supplies you with narcotics.'

On safer ground now I shook my head firmly.

'I fear, Detective Sergeant,' I said crisply, 'that
your accusation is baseless. Big Ahmed Patel is not
a bigamist.'

'What's your word for a man with four wives?'

'In fact, he has one wife, Mr Chisholm, and

*'I have tried to
stop you, Arthur
Daley, polluting
this patch with
your unlawful
activities'*
or
*'I'm going to put
the cuffs on you,
Arthur Daley'*

three mistresses. Patel is certainly a bit of a roué – too fond of the ladies perhaps. So he goes through a simple home-made ceremony with girls – and in spite of his size he is amazingly successful with the opposite sex – and calls them his little wives. But his so-called marriages have no legal significance. Looks like you haven't done your homework, Mr Chisholm. If you had, you'd know that neither Patel nor I have committed any crime but were just having a shared joke on the dog – on the phone.'

Out of the corner of my eye, I saw Terry to whom, unperceived by Chisholm, I had been signalling with very slight nods, ease away towards the back door in order to brief Patel as to what he should say when Chisholm called round. It was only an added precaution because every word I had said to the sleuth had been the truth – with one small exception. I had known for some time that Patel was not really a bigamist – but I had not yet found an opportunity to pass the good news on to him. He and his wives, therefore, would still be under the impression that their crowded household was outside the law of the land.

Chisholm was eyeing me narrowly.

'I can soon check this out, Daley –'

'Of course you can. And I trust you will. And I would not consider it inappropriate if, having done so, you was to return and tender me an apology for your damaging accusation.'

Chisholm's eyes narrowed while his mouth widened into a mirthless grin, producing an eerie and unpleasant effect. When he spoke it was quite softly at first but then on a rising note.

'You feel an apology would be appropriate, do you, Mr Daley? Simply because, as a properly appointed law-enforcement officer, I have for years done my best to clean up this patch which largely means attempting to stop you, Arthur Daley, from polluting it with your unlawful activities. I have a file on you which proves that you are the greatest single malefactor that Fulham has ever suffered. At least in modern times. It reveals, for example, that it was you who were responsible for the Birch Street electrical goods robberies, the break-ins in the Mitcham Terrace area and at least twenty-five other serious, and thus far unsolved, crimes that have been perpetrated since I joined this force. Now, in despair, I suppose that it is just possible that you are once again set to evade justice by means of a technicality but sooner or later I'm going to put the cuffs on you, Arthur Daley. And after that I will at long last get the reward I have been praying for through all these years of frustrated endeavour. I will sit in court and hear a judge utter those words with a sound like a great amen: 'Arthur Daley, I sentence you to serve not less than one million years in prison.'

As he reached this ringing conclusion Chisholm's eyes shone with an unholy light and he raised his clenched fists as if preparing to smite an evildoer. Then he gave a quick shrug and recovered his normal icy composure. Turning, he strode smartly towards the door, pausing only to snap, without turning round: 'Jones, do I take it you no longer wish to accompany me on my sordid rounds?' At these words, his Welsh side kick gave a start, turned and then shuffled out after what I had suddenly, and for the first time, perceived was his dangerously unhinged boss.

As all who know me well will testify, I am normally the most sympathetic of men. Under most circumstances I would have been deeply saddened to perceive that even such a doubtful asset to the human race as this particular copper had gone round the twist. But his derangement had this time come somewhat too close to causing me

real aggro for such sentimental luxuries. I realised
at long last that Chisholm was in the grip of an irresistible compulsion to deprive me of my freedom.

Who could say how such a monstrous and
utterly depraved notion had come to germinate
in the mind of what should have been a relatively harmless, if persistently irritating, snooper?
Possibly the almost daily spectacle of me cruising
through Fulham in my shining Jaguar saloon, nodding to right and left with easy smiles for my
numerous fans, had been more than he could bear.
Perhaps the contrast between my ready charm and
confidence, my popularity, my lavish lifestyle and
the respect in which I was held by the entire parish,
as compared to his own furtive, ratlike existence,
had caused Chisholm to flip his lid. There is ultimately no way of finding out what sparked off this
mindless vendetta in what passed for the brain of
this particular rozzer. But what could not be denied
was that something had to be done about it. If not,
then sooner or later Chisholm would reach the
logical next stage of his dreadful mental disease.
Unable to obtain evidence, since none existed,
of my supposed criminal activities he would start
fabricating it. And while it might be argued that
it was unlikely that any pitiful falsehoods he could
invent would carry much weight with reasonable
jurors it was still not utterly unknown for spite
and clumsy malice to topple a truly noble spirit.
I therefore perceived that I would have to take
defensive action, and that very soon. But what, if
any, defensive action was available to me?

I suddenly recalled that Chisholm had just
threatened me with a file he claimed to have
about my criminal activities. Now this could not
possibly be an official file because even if such a
thing, as a result of past misunderstandings about
my perfectly legitimate business affairs, did exist

£ We agreed I would donate a pony to the Robert Peel Home for Distressed ex-Cons

there was no way it could contain many of the things that Chisholm had mentioned. He had, for example, spoken of the Birch Street electrical goods robberies but no official file could in any way link me to those capers. I happened to know that they had been perpetrated by one Dave 'Tubeman' Piper, a very thin tea-leaf who specialised in effecting entries through ducts and suchlike which no normal-sized bloke could get through. This dishonest fellow was occasionally to be seen about the Winchester Club, brought there by a jovial member for a joke. In fact, we club members often permit the occasional rogue or other entertaining eccentric to come amongst us for an evening just for laughs. And that is how I knew that the 'Tubeman' had been the guilty party in the Birch Street jobs. The impertinent fellow had actually had the infernal cheek to try and sell me a load of electric irons, hairdriers and suchlike at ludicrous prices and I had of course realised that they must be the loot from the Birch Street caper. Naturally I indignantly sent the dishonest bloke packing with a flea in his ear. But now I was glad of the incident since I knew that it proved I could not be on any official record in connection with Birch Street. It followed therefore that Chisholm's file on me, which I believed was real, must be a private file that he himself had compiled. Needless to say I was not in the least alarmed at the thought of what it might contain since my probity was above reproach. But it did occur to me that it might be a good idea to have a look at this diseased compilation since it might help me to defend myself against Chisholm's lunatic obsession.

But could I get at it? Here again, if I had indeed been the crook that Chisholm had insanely persuaded himself that I was, the answer to that question would have been easy. I would simply have commissioned some tea-leaf to nip round to the cop's lair and nick it for me. But as an honest man, this path was clearly not available. And then a most strange and wonderful sequence of events took place which would be enough to convince a superstitious person that there is indeed a providence which watches out for innocent victims and keeps them from harm.

What happened was a bit like the famous historical story of the king of England who was being given a hard time by a friend who had made it to the top and become Archbishop of Canterbury. One day the king was having a couple of jars with some mates and, after a few meads possibly, shook his head sadly and remarked: 'Thomas (which was the name of the Archbishop) keeps obstructing my plans to make England a better place in which to live and bring up a family. I'd certainly reward anyone who could persuade him to belt up.' Now what King Henry meant, of course, was couldn't someone go and reason with the Archbishop and make him see that he was out of line. But those was very primitive times and a couple of knights, who were probably even more Brahms than the king himself, thought they saw a chance of making a dishonest bob or two. They staggered out of the boozing hall, climbed unsteadily onto their chargers and went pounding away to Canterbury where they found Thomas in his cathedral. Without a moment's hesitation they unshipped their swords and hacked the unfortunate priest into hamburger. A gory and terrible tale, you will be thinking, and you will be right. But it is nevertheless one that has certain strange similarities with the last act in the long struggle between Chisholm and me.

It began with me moaning loudly about my persecution by the rabid rozzer while taking my evening voddy and slimline down the Winchester.

Thinking I was just addressing Dave, and unaware that a tea-leaf called Mike the Maggot was seated on a barstool just two seats away with ears flapping, I told my old chum all about my suspicious that Chisholm had put together a fictitious file about me. I sighed and said:

'I'd give a lot to get a butcher's at that file.'

And something like one hour later I was doing just that.

'But where on earth did you get this?' I queried in dismay when Mike the Maggot, after beckoning me into a secluded corner of the club, laid it on the table before me.

'Where do you fink, Arthur?' he asked in his quaint Cockney accent. 'In Chisholm's bedroom, where else?'

'You mean you stole it?' I cried, aghast.

'Oh no. I just stood in the front door and whistled and it came bounding over to me with tail wagging.'

I pushed the sheaf of papers towards him.

'Return it at once!' I ordered sternly.

'No point, is there? That's only a photostat what I made for you. I already returned the original. Sweet as evaporated milk, it was. He'll never suspect it's been out of his drum.'

I shook my head vehemently.

'Then burn it. Place it in a public refuse bin. You should know, Maggot, that I cannot condone theft.'

'You don't have to condone it, Arthur. Just stump up the pony you promised for it.'

'I beg your pardon!' I exclaimed indignantly.

'I'eard you say you'd give a pony to get your hands on it.'

'Rubbish! What I actually said was that it was phoney and I washed my hands of it.'

'Oh, right. I must 'ave mis'eard. But any old

how, Arfur, you might as well have a quick butcher's since it's 'ere. The Old Bill's been giving you a 'ard time and you deserve the chance to defend yourself from false alegations.'

I had to concede there was truth in these words but I made it clear that I could not connive at Maggot's nefarious act. So we agreed that I would donate a pony to the Robert Peel Home for Distressed ex-Cons. I gave the money to the Maggot to donate for me and off he went with it.'

That night I sat up late poring over that almost incredible document. If I had committed a tenth of the crimes that Chisholm had put me down for I would have been too busy to eat or sleep never mind to run my complex business affairs. But it was not just the false accusations that made me gasp. It was the wild fantasy which caused a shiver to run down my spine at the realisation of how great a volcano of madness can be bubbling away beneath the surface of your common or garden

The Krays don't look nothing like me

Sergeant Plod.

Chisholm had no talent for drawing, but that hadn't stopped him from trying. Here and there in the file were crude representations of your present author in the guise of some of the more celebrated villains of both fact and fiction: Arthur Daley as Al Capone, Arthur Daley as Fagin, Arthur Daley as a Kray, even Arthur Daley as Professor Moriarty. There was also a crude cartoon, just recognisable as me from the cigar and the sympathetic smile which had survived even Chisholm's attempts to make it seem like an evil leer, as a huge spider poised at the centre of a crime web that radiated out beyond Fulham and even England to the four corners of the earth. And yet you will be astonished to learn that when I finally reached the end of this distressing document, a great sense of peace came over me for I knew that my persecution was nearly at an end. All that remained was to arrange a meet with Detective Sergeant Chisholm at some discreet spot.

We finally settled on a bench facing the river beside the grounds of the Bishop's Palace. It was a spot which was not only discreet but beautiful. As I sat waiting for Chisholm to show, and never doubting that he would, I suddenly had a kind of vision. I glanced along the path, lightly frequented by mums pushing prams and old men tottering with sticks, and suddenly saw a schoolboy bowling a hoop towards me and, as he approached, I heard the startling wail of an air-raid siren. For a moment or two I felt fear and then I realised that I was looking, and listening, back half a century and that the lad in knickerbockers was me.

'Arthur Daley,' grated a voice like two icebergs colliding, 'you are not obliged to say anything but since you've dragged me all the way out here I'll be bloody pissed off if you don't.'

Nor does Al Capone

I realised that this must be the kind of joke with which cops convulse each other in their locker rooms but I felt far too serene to care.

'Oh, hello, Mr Chisholm, good of you to join me.'

'Your invitation spoke of something that might be to my advantage,' proclaimed the knife-featured sleuth, seating himself beside me on the bench and gazing straight ahead.

'Nice spot this, Mr Chisholm,' I pointed out.

'Sheer bliss. But I do hope, Arthur, that you haven't disrupted my morning's task of rounding up criminals just to admire the view?'

'Not at all, Mr Chisholm. I was just wondering if you'd find your next posting anything like as attractive.'

'No idea, Arthur. But since I have no intention of policing any other portion of England for the foreseeable future it doesn't matter a great deal, does it?'

'It could happen sooner than you think.'

'Are you trying to tell me something, Daley?'

'Could be. Now, do you want to pat me for wires?'

'So that when you offer me five grand to apply for a move I'll know it's not a frame-up? I have no need to establish that you're clean, Arthur. You see, if you offered me ten thousand or twenty thousand, or even the legendary treasure of the Incas, to do a bunk, I'd tell you to get stuffed. I intend to stay right here until I get the evidence to put you away. Mere money could never recompense me for missing that.'

I sighed and shook my head, watching a skiff full of young Oxford scholars, or perhaps Cambridge ones, straining at the oars.

'I do have it in mind to offer you something tempting, Sergeant Chisholm. But it's not

Nor does Fagin, at least as played by Sir John Lawrence Guinness

money.'

'I'm all agog, Arthur.'

I was surprised to find that, as I stooped to open my briefcase, which was nestling between my feet, I felt a slight touch of pity for the hapless rozzer. He had no suspicion of the fury that was about to hit him.

'This is what I planned to offer you, Mr Chisholm,' I said affably as I placed on his lap a copy of his illicit file on me.

He gazed down at it without moving for a moment. Then he frowned very slightly, obviously puzzled rather than worried, and tapped the document lightly with his forefinger. Only then did he look round at me.

'Where did you get this?' he asked.

'Bloke I know. Thought it might interest me. No idea how he got his hands on it. It is yours isn't it, Sergeant? I mean I've checked the handwriting against various, mainly threatening, communications I've had from you over the years.'

'Oh, it's mine alright. And I'm grateful to you for returning it to me. Very public-spirited of you. Is that all you wanted with me, Arthur?'

I confess that I was a little surprised by his continued nonchalance. I hastily continued:

'It is not. Now what you're holding is a photostat, Mr Chisholm. I'm surprised you didn't spot that.'

'But I did spot it, Arthur. A good detective registers such details with the same ease he breathes air.'

'Then you will doubtless realise that there could be other photostats of it elsewhere?'

He nodded affably.

'I suppose there could. And I don't mind in the least. If it gives you pleasure to store copies of my diligent homework be my guest. And now, Arthur,

there are thieves waiting to be nabbed, brasses to
be booked, possibly even murderers –'

I began to feel just a shade anxious.

'You're not getting the message, Sergeant Chisholm. I am here to propose an amicable bargain.'

'Then propose it, Arthur, and let's get it over.
My delight in your society is beginning to wane.'

'The terms are as follows,' I said earnestly.
'You will apply for a transfer to some other force
and, until it comes through, you will totally cease
harassing me. I, in exchange, will not bring this
clandestine file to the attention of your superior
officer, Detective Chief-Superintendant Cuthbert
Basildon.'

Chisholm stared at me bleakly.

'I am at a loss, Arthur, to understand your
reasoning. Why should I object to your displaying
evidence of my diligence and concern for law-
enforcement to my superior?'

I swallowed.

'This file shows that you have a disturbed mind,
Sergeant Chisholm.'

'Very likely. Who wouldn't have a disturbed
mind consorting with you lot every blessed working day. Arthur, all cops have disturbed minds and
some of the very best have deeply disturbed ones.
Mind you, on the evidence of this meeting I'd say
your mind easily outranks any disturbed police one
I've ever encountered. Now go peddle your hooky
goods, Arthur, because –'

I held up my hand for silence.

'It is clear, Sergeant Chisholm, that you are not
ashamed to have the product of your deranged fantasies paraded before your seniors. Shocking, I call
it, but possibly understandable. Before you depart,
however, I suggest you glance at page seventeen.'

'How do you mean?'

'Permit me.'

I took the volume from his lap and turned to the page I had specified. This was easy to do because it had a white card marking the place. There were, in fact, ten other such cards scattered about in the document.

'Ready?' I asked.

'For what?' queried Chisholm, clearly genuinely puzzled.

'For having your memory unpleasantly jogged. I would wager a barrel of rum to a pair of rusty handcuffs that you've forgotten you ever penned this passage, Sergeant. It's in a section where you, without a single shred of evidence, speculate as to whether I might have been involved in a caper involving forged police notepaper. It reads, in part, as follows: "On the other hand it is conceivable that Daley did not steal the notepaper but that it was supplied by Batty Basildon himself. I have once or twice caught the Chief Super and Daley exchanging a glance when Daley has been brought in for questioning. It is quite possible that they are in cahoots. After all, where did Batty get the money for the new Mercedes he's been swanking about in? There are other little things I've noticed that have from time to time suggested to me that Batty is that most repugnant of beings, a bent copper."'

I glanced round and saw that Chisholm was apparently frowning at a bus crawling in heavy traffic along the embankment on the far side of the river. His lips seemed pressed together rather tightly.

'Still quite bucked at the thought of your guvnor getting a butcher's?' I asked softly.

I could see his abnormally large (often the sign of the copper) adam's apple bob like a bottle in a heavy sea. But he nodded slightly.

'And why not? A good detective is not limited, in his search for the truth, by considerations of diplomacy. The Chief Super –'

'You mean good old Batty?'

'Daley, the deputy mayor, who was at school with my boss, has, in my presence, used that very nickname.'

'Ah, but you didn't happen to be at Winchester with Old Batty, did you, Sergeant?'

With an obvious effort, Chisholm turned and looked me full in the face.

'You still don't understand, Daley. I have nothing to fear. My integrity is as seamless as an actor's ego. So I will now take my departure and leave you –'

'That was just for openers, Mr Chisholm. It gets better. You'll love next bit.'

I turned swiftly to another page marked by a card and read:

'"I am now convinced that Basildon is part of an information swapping gang that includes several other heads of CID in London. There is no doubt whatsoever that Basildon feeds Daley and other notorious local villains with information in exchange for" – you said something, Sergeant?'

'No. I didn't say anything, Daley. Not a thing. Er – you intimate that there are other copies of this – this – perhaps somewhat indiscreet document?'

'Yes, three. Oh, here's another good passage. You'll cheer when you hear it.'

He broke on the sixth extract. I had just started reading:

'"I have thus proved beyond any shadow of doubt that Batty Basildon –"'

'Stop calling him that!'

'I'm not. You are, Sergeant.'

'Then stop reading it. All right – all right – you win. The words are like burning embers in my mouth but – you win, Daley. I'll go. Oh the pity of it. Enough crime in Fulham – even without

To-day Fulham, tomorrow the world

your contribution, Daley – to keep the greediest detective in business for a lifetime and just because of a few casual jottings –'

'I know,' I sympathised. 'Life's tough. But you'll find crime in your next posting too, Sergeant. It's everywhere, like the Old Bill.'

There was quite a long pause and then, in a choked and broken whisper, Chisholm began:

'I suppose – you wouldn't consider – well, I've got some savings and –'

'Easy, Sergeant,' I broke in quickly. 'You never did pat me for wires, remember? No, we've made our deal. The photostats in exchange for your departure for even blacker scenes of sin elsewhere.'

He gave a long sigh.

'Have you got all the copies with you?'

'Let's not play silly buggers, Sergeant. I'll post them to you. To your new address. But we'll both always know, won't we, that you can never be completely sure that there's not just one more in existence.'

'Daley, you –'

'No animosity, Sergeant. And before we part for good, I'd just like to make it clear that you always had me wrong. I'm not a crook. I'm a businessman. And – Sergeant – it's been a real pleasure doing business with you.'

He gazed at me for a moment like a starving wolf and then his teeth showed briefly in a bleak smile. An instant later and he rose and strode rapidly away along the river bank without a backwards glance – coat, shoes, stride, everything about him crying out: I'm a copper in plain clothes but don't let on that you've spotted it. I watched him out of sight and then I sighed and leaned back in my seat as I fumbled in my breast pocket for a cigar. It really was a glorious day on the river.